Strange Magic

Edited by Catherine Jordan

SUNBURY PRESS
Mechanicsburg, PA USA

Published by Sunbury Press, Inc.
Mechanicsburg, Pennsylvania

www.sunburypress.com

NOTE: This is a work of fiction. Names, characters, places and incidents are the product of the author's imagination or are used fictitiously, and any resemblance to actual persons, living or dead, business establishments, events or locales is entirely coincidental.

For information about special discounts for bulk purchases, please contact Sunbury Press Orders Dept. at (855) 338-8359 or orders@sunburypress.com.

To request one of our authors for speaking engagements or book signings, please contact Sunbury Press Publicity Dept. at publicity@sunburypress.com.

ISBN: 978-1-62006-849-6 (Trade paperback)
ISBN: 978-1-62006-850-2 (Mobipocket)

Library of Congress Control Number: 2016961798

FIRST SUNBURY PRESS EDITION: December 2016

Product of the United States of America
0 1 1 2 3 5 8 13 21 34 55

Set in Bookman Old Style
Designed by Crystal Devine
Cover by Lawrence Knorr
Edited by Allyson Gard

Continue the Enlightenment!

Contents

Foreword

In the late 1980s, I wrote a nifty little novel and signed on with a veteran agent who peddled it all over New York City.

I papered the wall of my office with scores of rejection letters, licked my wounds, and went on to other pursuits. But I always wondered why my story went nowhere.

Fast forward thirty years. In collaboration with the **Perry County Council of the Arts**, author Don Helin assembled a stellar faculty of successful, published authors to teach A Novel Idea, a year-long class for aspiring novelists. I signed on for that first year, half to represent **PCCA**, and half hoping I might learn what I did wrong three decades ago.

A Novel Idea didn't disappoint. I learned many reasons why my book never got out of the starting blocks, all the time wishing I could have avoided these pitfalls by taking such a course before I ever started writing.

But there was an unanticipated bonus. My 18 classmates demonstrated a gift for the written word that made each session a joy. As they read aloud the fruits of their writing exercises, I marveled at their talent and inspiration. They made me laugh, pulled hard at my emotions, or transported me to places that I had never been.

That is why I was so excited when author and facilitator Catherine Jordan and publisher Lawrence Knorr approached us with the idea of this anthology. I wanted to read the tales that my peers, and those from the class that followed, had to spin. Please relish them with the knowledge that they were written by ordinary people who believed they had a story to tell and had the courage to start writing.

—Rog Smith, executive director
Perry County Council of the Arts

Jon,

Thank you for opening my heart to Angels. My "early days" at the Inner-Connection were key to opening the Pathway to writing. I'll never forget my first angel class with Candy Glanzis with the "guest speaker," Uriel who overlooks creativity, "especially in writing!"

Brenda Andych

Introduction

Strange Magic conjures all sorts of thoughts and ideas, as it did with our group of writers. Take a step back and think about what it means to you. Do you think of the magic behind attractions, such as your first kiss, or your twenty year marriage? How about the strange realism inside a vivid dream, or surreal and fantastical worlds? The theme is more than a feeling, or an image, or a supernatural moment. And so are the stories within this collection.

This anthology was to be a collaboration between the writing facilitators and the aspiring students. A Novel Idea Workshop consists of a group of teachers who share their experience and love of the craft with a group of writers, while guiding them through the writing process. What better way to guide a student then to stroke their ideas, offer critiques, and steer them toward publication.

Within this compilation, not only will you find diverse genres, but you will also find that the students' stories have been wedged between the facilitators' stories. Each writer had one goal in mind—to tell a good story.

Thank you to each author who offered submissions and to our publisher, Lawrence Knorr, for this opportunity.

Happy reading!

—Catherine Jordan, editor

PAINT BY NUMBERS

by Maria V. Snyder

Kassandra sighed. Another math problem, and not a particularly pretty one at all; it reflected browns and grays. She glanced at the blank canvas on her easel with longing. Not now, her mother had said; finish the assignment and then you can paint.

A twinge of pain stabbed between her eyebrows. Planting her elbows on each side of the homework paper, she massaged her temples, making a teepee over the equation. A Laplace transform stared back at her. So tedious. Why was she doing differential equations when all her friends were struggling with calculus?

You have a gift, her mother's cold voice replied in her mind. Her mother acted so tense about mathematics all the time. Kassie wondered why—a full math scholarship to the local university was all but assured. Mom's aura used to be a soothing blue, but now a bright red flamed around her that seared into Kassie's eyes.

Kassie's gaze slid back to the canvas waiting in the corner of her bedroom near the double windows. Her paintings hung on every inch of wall space, they were piled on the floor and stacked on her dresser—only her twin bed and desk remained clear. Okay, so maybe she was a bit obsessed. But the potential of that white space called to her. It was her headache release. The only time the pain stopped was when she surrendered to the colors and painted.

With effort, she refocused on the math problem. She grabbed a pencil and wrote all the steps to the answer. Heaven forbid if she skipped steps. She gasped with mock horror. How would Mom ever know if she really did the work and didn't just Google it?

Her mood improved as she worked through the calculations. The problem became prettier as she moved through it. There were lots of twos. Twos were aquamarine, and the solution promised more color. Taking a break, Kassie stared absently at the easel. She wouldn't have time to paint tonight. Then a compromise jumped into her mind. Perhaps she could do both.

Excited by the idea, Kassie went to her computer and activated her color software. She placed a clean palette under the dispenser. The dispenser was made of a ring of thin metal tubes with rubber nipples on the ends. Each tube contained a specific color of paint, and, when guided by the computer, the nipple spat out a measured portion onto the palette.

The dispenser had been a gift from her father when his laboratory had updated to the latest model. He needed the newest equipment since he was a well-known fertility expert with an unprecedented ninety percent conception rate. A surge of pride warmed her chest. Without his skills with in vitro fertilization, she wouldn't have been born. And he was famous enough to have distracters. Other fertility doctors claimed his work was immoral, yet her dad has never been investigated. Funny how jealousy and back-stabbing wasn't confined to high school.

Despite her mother's chagrin, Kassie had been thrilled over the dispenser. Her father knew how she hated to mix colors with a paintbrush, how hard it was to precisely match them. Once programmed, the dispenser consistently solved this problem, mixing the exact colors she needed for her paintings.

She punched the math equation into the computer. The dispenser spun and doled out quarter-sized gobs of paint. When the palette was full, Kassie painted the math problem on her canvas. Back and forth from canvas to computer, Kassie worked on the Laplace transform, painting the colors of the numbers and symbols. Colors only she could see.

Kassie was so engrossed in her painting that she didn't hear her bedroom door open.

"Kassandra Reed," her mother said. Her voice was as tight as last year's fashions. "Is your homework done?"

"Almost," Kassie said. She bit the end of her paintbrush as her mother walked to the desk.

"You've barely started." Her mother's expression hardened.

The danger signs were there: tense muscles, hands glued to hips, pressed lips, and spine as straight as a highway in Kansas. Kassie chose her words with as much care as she chose her paintbrushes. "I'm painting the math problem. See?" She pointed to the canvas. Only one line left to paint and it would be complete. To Kassie it was clear. She walked over to the desk and wrote the answer in pencil. "A compromise."

"You did what?" Confusion bunched her mother's eyebrows together. They hovered over her small blue eyes.

Kassie tried to explain. But as storm clouds thickened around her mother's head, she knew she was in for a full gale. A reminder—as if she could forget—of how much her mother disliked the fact that she saw colored numbers, how she believed it flawed Kassie's gift. This painting was throwing it into her mother's face.

"What's the matter?" Kassie's father asked from the doorway.

Thank infinity! Her dad stepped into the room, completely oblivious to Mom's four hundred-degree glare. Kassie showed him the painting, and demonstrated how it resolved the problem by filling in the last line.

"Clever," her father said. "Now what do you do with the picture?"

Kassie stepped back, considering. Despite the jumble of colors, there was a pattern. Using burnt sienna first then cobalt blue, she laced lines across the canvas.

"Two women?" her father asked. "No, wait, it's the same lady. A mirror image. That's great."

"No, it isn't," her mother said, freezing the smile on her dad's face. "She's supposed to be doing her homework."

"But—" Kassie tried.

Thrusting the math paper into her hands, her mother said, "Do it the right way, now. And you're grounded for a week for this little stunt."

"Fine," Kassie said, slamming the paper down on her desk. "It won't make any difference to me. I've been technically grounded for the last seventeen years because you won't let me have a job, drive, or go out with my friends. All you let me do is math." She spat the words at her mother.

"In that case, no painting for a week."

Stunned, Kassie gaped at her.

"I thought that would shut your smart mouth." Her mother left the room.

Kassie turned to her father, but he clicked into helpless henpecked mode and followed Mom. Frustrated anger consumed her, and she stabbed the pencil into the painting. It broke and her hand smeared the still wet picture. She tried three more pencils before her temper fizzled and her headache returned with a vengeance. Sighing, she washed her hands in her bathroom—adding more colored flecks to the once-white basin.

Back at her desk, she worked on the math problem. An hour later, a strange warmth brushed her skin, interrupting her concentration. The air in the room thickened with the heavy scent of smoke. The light in her bedroom dimmed as the furniture blurred and spun. A migraine induced delusion? Kassie no longer sat at her computer desk. Instead she was at an old rolled-top desk. Candlelight shone on a leather journal spread open in front of her. The thick pages were filled with complex mathematical equations. An open bottle of black ink was on the right side with one of those strange metal pens lying next to it.

Kassie froze, taking in a few deep breaths to steady her out-of-control heart. The oily aroma of melted wax filled her nose as the smoke stung her eyes. Her bedroom had transformed into some old-fashioned nightmare. Was that an abacus? And a protractor? They replaced her computer and cellphone. The candles lined the top of the desk.

This had to be an illusion. Kassie touched a flame. She jerked her hand back as the heat singed her fingers. The pain jolted her from the vision and her bedroom solidified around her.

Sucking on her fingers, Kassie scanned the room. Everything remained the same. No creepy desk. But what about her red skin? The candle had stood where her desk light was, she must have burnt her fingers on the bulb.

It had to be stress. Right? She was exhausted and emotionally drained. Was that a psychotic break? Did teenagers get them? Afraid the strange vision would return, Kassie finished her homework in record time and crawled into bed.

That night her sleep was troubled by dreams of an endless parade of kaleidoscopic numbers. They marched by in wave after wave. When she woke up in a cold sweat at three a.m., she choked back tears. She couldn't escape the pressure even in her dreams.

***

The next day, Kassie couldn't focus on Professor Millen's lecture. She was preoccupied by the black-haired, Herculean god named Zeckland who sat one row down and two seats over from her. The best part of having to sit through a college math class was the college men. They were not like the boys at her high school at all.

After attending her high school classes in the morning, she rode the public bus downtown to Longshore University. She'd arrived early just so she could listen to Zeckland and his friends gossip and boast while she pretended to study her textbook. They ignored her as usual as they draped themselves on the desks near her seat. She imagined taking Zeckland to her senior prom. Every girl in her school would drool with envy.

"A perfect paper as always, Miss Reed." Professor Millen's comment jerked her from her daydream as he handed her the latest test.

The other students stared at her. Fire spread across her cheeks as the desire to slide under her desk pulsed in her chest. She wished the professor would stop commenting on her scores each time. If he was trying to shame the other students into doing better, it wasn't working. Most of the glances were laced with poison; she had blown the curve again.

After class, Kassie waited for her mother to pick her up at the student union café. Normally, she would retreat to the library, but today she had no desire to surround herself with quiet. Instead, she found an empty table in the back corner. When she finished her differential equations homework, she pulled out her sketchbook. No painting didn't mean no drawing. Besides, the avid faces of the students grouped together around the café inspired her. They glowed with life and passion as they talked.

She drew portraits and compared them to her own features. Her straight nose matched her poker straight hair, which hung down her back. With blond hair and blue eyes, Kassie didn't resemble either her mother or father, who both had brown hair and eyes. She actually resembled her great-great-grandmother of all people. Her mother showed her an old photograph of a woman with the same oval face and high cheekbones as Kassie's.

One particularly noisy group grabbed her attention. It was Zeckland and his friends. They caught her staring. Mortified, she ducked her head behind her sketchbook.

After a minute, she peeked out. The guys were headed straight for her. Panicked, she stuffed the sketchbook into her backpack, and concentrated on her homework, trying to appear calm despite the fact that her arms and legs had just gone numb.

"Hey, it's Miss Perfect Paper Reed," Zeckland said.

Kassie glanced up into his blue eyes. A smile softened his words. He wore jeans, black cowboy boots with silver accents, black T-shirt, a silver necklace with a cross, and a black leather jacket. And he was surrounded by a purple aura. In other words, he was perfection incarnated.

She forced sound through her tight throat. "It's Kass."

He introduced himself and his two friends, Levi and Riley. Levi's aura was a midnight blue, and Riley's was brown flecked with copper. Without invitation, Zeckland sat across from her as the others dragged chairs from nearby tables. Kassie kept forgetting to breathe as Zeckland ordered her a coffee. Sleek confidence oozed from his every gesture.

"Finished already?" he asked, pulling her homework toward him.

She nodded, unable to talk for fear of embarrassing herself.

"Man." He shook his head. "This is a tough one and you managed to complete it in . . ." He looked at his cellphone. "Half an hour."

Levi and Riley whistled in appreciation. Sudden feeling returned to her limbs as hot fire raced along her skin. They removed their differential equation textbooks and paper from their backpacks.

"We're having a hard time with this class. Perhaps you could help us?" Zeckland asked.

Kassie stared at him for a moment in shock. "Sure."

"Dr. Millen the villain," Levi said as he wrote the homework problem on his sheet. "Ancient, dinosaur guy, won't let us use our laptops. I haven't used a pencil in years."

"The pointy end goes down," Riley teased.

The coffee arrived and, as the guys worked on the math, Kassie took a tentative sip. The strong bitter taste flooded her mouth. When she looked around the café, everything had a maroon tinge to it as if she had just donned a pair of red sunglasses. It was kinda cool and strange at the same time.

Then another vision descended. The café turned into a large classroom with chalkboards on stands. Equations covered the boards. She sat with a number of men dressed in strange formal suits. They occupied a wooden conference table, drinking coffee and discussing mathematics.

Before she panicked, Kassie gulped her drink. The hot liquid seared her throat and restored her to the present.

Zeckland and his friends were concentrating on their books. If they noticed any odd behavior from her, they didn't show it. Relieved, she leaned back. Occasionally, they stopped to ask Kassie a question, or to look at her paper for guidance. She also noticed they were easily distracted by any female that entered or left the café.

Their auras flickered and dulled at times. Usually Kassie liked to study auras. By the way the light moved and flashed around someone, Kassie could determine quite a bit about that person's personality. But after that crazy vision, she was quite distracted.

"Hey, Zeck," Riley said. "Don't forget the Hex Girls are playing tonight at the Gaff."

"Happy hour starts at six. If we don't go early we'll never get a table," Levi said.

Zeckland glanced at his phone. "There's plenty of time, unless you guys need dates, then there isn't enough time in the world."

"At least we're not secretly in love with the Hex Girls' drummer," Riley said. "Oh, Veruke," he continued in a high-pitched voice. "You're the heartbeat of the band, your drumsticks fly like the wind."

Riley and Levi laughed while Zeckland shook his head.

"Children," Zeckland said disdainfully to Kassie. "I'd ask you to come along, but you're the youngest looking freshman I've seen. Unless you got a killer fake ID, there's no way the bouncers will let you in."

"That's okay. I already have plans." Delighted that he believed she was a college freshman, she tried to sound sophisticated and worldly even though her plans included being grounded and alone in her bedroom.

"Maybe next time," Zeckland said.

And it was the possibility of next time that had Kassie's full attention as the guys finished their papers, packed up and said goodbye. The possibility of next time made her late meeting her mother and allowed her to blissfully ignore her mother's griping on the way home.

Except when Mom declared, "I'm signing you up for two college classes next semester."

Startled from her happy place, she asked, "Which ones?"

"Differential equations 201, and Physics 104. They're both late afternoon classes, so you won't miss any school."

How about missing her life? "Can I take an art class instead of physics?" She tried just for the sake of trying.

"No. You don't *need* art classes."

"But I *want* to take art. Doesn't that matter? Perhaps I'll meet someone else who sees colors."

"That's enough, Kassandra. This art thing is just a hobby. I won't have this . . . this . . . synesthesia . . ." Her mom said the word like she was pulling a hair from her mouth. ". . . interfering with your math studies."

Well, that was progress. Her mother had actually spoken the name of Kassie's neurological phenomena aloud. Synesthesia. "But—"

"No more. How can you whine when you have been given this gift? I would have killed for your talents. Everything I ever did in my life was average. No matter what I tried or how hard I practiced or studied the results were always the same. Average." Kassie's mother gripped the steering wheel hard, staring straight ahead. "You were doing long division at age four. You're destined to become a great mathematician. How can you waste your gift by wanting to paint?" Her mother pulled the car into the garage.

Kassie jerked the car door open. "It's not a gift. It's a curse." She slammed the door and ran to her room.

***

Kassie was working on her homework when her father brought her dinner and a present.

"What's this?" Kassie asked as she opened the bag. She pulled out a CD, and turned it over in her hands. She didn't recognize the name on the label. "Michael Torke?"

"He's a New York composer. His compositions were inspired by his synesthesia. See the names?"

Kassie read the song titles. Bright Blue Music. Yellow Page.

"I thought you might like it. You know, a kindred spirit."

"Thanks," she said without much enthusiasm.

Her father sighed and studied her for a while. He eventually left, but he startled her when he returned with his medical bag.

"I'm fine," she insisted.

For once he was stern. "You're jumpy and irritable," he said.

He performed a quick check of her vitals. "Any problems? Headaches? Stomach pains? Dizziness? Trouble sleeping?"

Kassie answered no to all of them even though her head pounded and she had nightmares. Not to mention those strange visions. If she admitted that, her mother would get involved. And that would give Mom another thing to nag her about. Did you take your pills? How did you sleep? And on and on.

"You look tired, Sweets. Promise me you'll go to bed early the next couple of nights?"

"I promise, Daddy."

When her father left, Kassie changed into her Dr. Who pajamas. Determined to keep her promise, she hoped it would help ease the guilt over lying to her father. Kassie slid her new CD into her computer and turned the speaker volume low. Perhaps the music would help soothe her dreams. It worked for awhile. Colored bubbles drifted in her mind. Then equations grew inside the bubbles, expanding the soapy spheres until they popped, numbers rained down on her.

As she raced to solve the equations, monstrous dogs with sharp silver teeth pursued her. If she slowed down, they would consume her.

***

Professor Millen's class was more enjoyable now that Zeckland, Levi and Riley sat next to Kassie. Instead of having to eavesdrop on their conversations, she was now included in them. For several weeks, Kassie and her new friends sat together for class, then ambled over to the café for coffee and to work on their homework. And best of all, no more creepy visions.

She had painted a portrait of Zeckland using the colors of the letters in his name. The first letter of any word tended to taint the following letters. Since Kassie saw Z as black with gold flecks, the other letters leaned toward the jewel tones. The portrait rendered his image with gold-flecked black hair, sapphire eyes, ruby lips, and amber skin.

Studying Zeckland at the café, Kassie thought her painting had captured his inner essence, and it was her favorite project to date.

For the first time in a long while, Kassie enjoyed math. Math had been fun until her mother had turned into the mathematics police. Mom never discussed anything else with her. Kassie couldn't understand why. It wasn't like she was preparing for the Olympics or that there was a deadline. Why couldn't she learn differential equations when she was actually in college? Far away from her mother.

When Professor Millen handed out their third test paper with his usual comments, instead of receiving hostile stares, she received broad smiles from her friends. Zeckland was in good spirits as Kassie's tutoring had paid off. He and his buddies had gotten high scores on their tests, but their auras flickered as if something wasn't quite right. They were probably just worried about the next test.

Two thirds of the way into the semester, Professor Millen surprised the class. "I know the syllabus said there will be four tests and a final, but in lieu of the fourth test I want you to write a paper on a mathematician. Call it a mini-biography. I want ten to twelve pages, double-spaced. And no researching on the Internet. I want you to have actual book references. Here." He emailed the class the details of the assignment.

The students groaned audibly.

"What does he think he's doing?" Levi whispered. "Math professors don't assign term papers."

"Especially not when the semester's almost over," Riley said.

"Someone should complain to the dean. Millen's not thinking with all his primary numbers," Levi said.

"Quiet, guys," Zeckland ordered. "It'll be easy. A break from solving problems and none of the hassle of studying for a test."

After class, Riley and Levi complained all the way to the library, but Zeckland seemed upbeat.

"Did you have a mathematician in mind?" Kassie asked Zeckland.

"I was thinking about Laplace. You know, the transform guy? Except that's all I know about him."

"Marquis Pierre Simon de Laplace, French mathematician and astronomer, 1749 to 1827."

"Friend of yours?" Zeckland teased.

"Distant cousin," she said.

As Zeckland laughed, Kassie watched his purple aura brighten around him. When the four of them entered the library, the guys gawked like tourists.

"Don't tell me," Kassie said. "You've never been to the library?"

Three identical guilty looks flashed her way. She groaned.

"It's too quiet," Levi said.

"Too serious," Riley agreed.

"And they don't serve drinks," Zeckland said. "If you want me to frequent a place, it's gotta have a menu."

They giggled like children as Kassie led them to a hidden nook on the third floor. It was her favorite spot, since it was surrounded on three sides by bookcases.

To Kassie, the library was one giant stained glass window. Brilliant colors gleamed from all directions, and when no one was looking, she liked to turn a circle and watch the colors change and blend. It was just like being in the middle of a kaleidoscope.

Resisting the urge to spin, she searched for books on mathematicians. Computers had infiltrated every aspect of life, but the book still persevered. There was no comparison to the sensation of holding a physical book in hand, the clean smell of ink, and the smooth feel of the pages.

When she returned with a stack of biographies, Levi and Riley had no idea who they wanted to research so they let her pick. Choosing mathematicians for them was easy, but she had a harder time finding someone that interested her until she found a book on women mathematicians. Happy with her search, she headed back to the table.

As the guys read through their books, Kassie flipped the pages of her volume. It was unbelievable how many women had pursued math. Even back in the 1800's, there were some that had gotten a Ph.D. Not quite sure what she was looking for, Kassie scanned the pages.

An image flew off the page like an exploding rainbow. Strange since the old photo was faded and grainy. Underneath the picture was: Cora Bennel, 1886 to 1916. Kassie read through Cora's biography. Cora Bennel had gotten her Ph.D. in Mathematics in 1912. And she had been a painter. Perfect.

Over the next week Kassie researched Cora. During that time, a strong feeling of familiarity nagged at her. All of Kassie's extended family either lived far away or were dead. But maybe, just maybe Cora was related to her. Poor Cora was thirty years old when she died in a fire, but she could have had a child. Perhaps she was a three times removed cousin or very distant aunt—one could hope. It would explain why Kassie had a gift for numbers. And just be really cool.

At dinner a couple of nights before the paper was due, she asked her parents about the old photograph of her great-great-grandmother her dad had shown her when she was little.

Her mother frowned. A forkful of mashed potatoes frozen in mid-air. "Why do you need it?"

Only one answer would appease her mother. "It's for school."

Glancing at her father, Mom asked, "Do you still have all those old photos?"

"Yes, but what's it for?" her father asked.

"We're learning genetics in science. You know, dominate and recessive genes. Stuff like that." She shrugged, downplaying her interest.

"What about us?" He pointed his knife at Mom. "We're closer."

"Mr. Schaffer said to bring a photo from our oldest relative."

He looked at Kassie with his thoughtful face, but Mom didn't seem bothered by the request. A role reversal. But he finally agreed. After dinner, she trailed him to his office.

"I hope you know that I can answer any questions you might have about genetics." He gave her a self-deprecating smile. "I am the expert."

She paused at the entrance to the room. "You're not going to *try* to explain the birds and bees to me again . . . are you?" Kassie pressed her hands to her chest in mock horror.

"I'm never going to live that down am I?" he asked.

"Nope." Kassie wove her way through the messy piles of books and papers on the floor. How did he find anything? Colors popped and flowed around her feet. The room smelled of his cologne—Old Spice. She flopped on the leather armchair in front of his desk. "I did learn one thing from that talk, though."

"Really?" Her father rummaged in the closet.

"Yeah. I learned the definition of unmitigated disaster." Her mother had used that phrase quite a few times while laughing on the phone with her friends.

"Funny." His dry tone indicated he was not amused. He sat behind his desk and passed her a wooden box. "This is her keepsake box. It's all I have so please be careful."

Kassie kept her expression neutral, but her heart tapped against her chest like an impatient toddler wanting attention. A flora design had been etched into the wood along with initials. C.B.R.

Her pulse sped up as she traced them. "What's her full name?"

"Catherine Benton Reed, my grandfather's mother. Benton was her maiden name."

Kassie wilted. So close. Oh well. She had known the odds weren't in her favor, but a girl could hope.

Her father's cell phone rang. He glanced at the display. "Sorry, it's a client. Dr. Reed speaking."

No wanting to hear about some lady's fertility problems, Kassie took the box to her bedroom. Sitting at her desk, she opened the lid. The photograph of Catherine rested on top. It was the one she remembered. Dressed in an old-fashioned ruffled gown, her hair was pulled up into one of those puffy buns that resemble a hat. Her great-great-grandmother looked to be about twenty or so, but it was hard to tell—everyone in those old photos appeared to be older due to their dour expressions. No doubt Kassie was related to the woman; they had the same cheekbones, pointy chin and forehead. Actually, Kassie looked more like Catherine now than when she was little.

A musty smell laced with wood smoke floated up when she removed the photo for a closer look. Underneath was a collection of tarnished jewelry, a few coins, a silver comb and a hairbrush with a couple blond strands still coiled around the bristles. At the bottom was a leather book. The journal was familiar. She searched her memories and remembered her first strange vision—the old-fashioned office with the book on the roll-top desk.

The room spun and the scent of wax threatened to dominate her senses. Determined not to have another hallucination, Kassie opened the journal. Equations lined the pages just like in the vision. Candlelight flickered on the edge of her vision.

No. Kassie concentrated on the numbers, recognizing the proofs and theorems. Was this Catherine's book or her husband's? At least someone else in the family enjoyed math. Calmer, Kassie flipped through the pages until the numbers ended and the colors began. Page after page of splotches of paint.

Another vision? Her cellphone remained in its charger. Whew. But as she stared at the colors, Kassie recognized the pattern. It was very similar to her Laplace transform painting. And if she concentrated . . . she could turn those colors into numbers.

Kassie pushed back from her desk. Did her great-great-grandmother have synesthesia as well as high cheekbones, an oval face, blond hair, and a love of math? That would be . . . too much of a coincidence.

She fingered the brittle blond strands on the hairbrush. A sick uneasy feeling swirled in her stomach. Kassie grabbed her backpack and pulled out her research book. The one with Cora Bennel's picture. Opening to Cora's section, Kassie studied the photograph, comparing it to Catherine's. Oval face, light-colored hair, high cheekbones. Kassie's gaze returned to the hair wound around the bristles. How long did DNA last? Her father would know. She gasped as a horrible, awful thought filled her head.

An unwelcome image of Kassie's father digging up a casket to retrieve DNA samples shuddered in her mind. Dr. Reed, the famous fertility doctor, with mud splattered on his lab coat. Mrs. Reed the average woman nagging for a special child. Dr. Reed risking his medical license and potential jail time for a math genius extraordinaire. Was Kassie a clone?

Was she only alive to serve her parent's goals? She wasn't an original work of art, but wearing borrowed skin, and remembering borrowed memories. Cora/Catherine's memories. At least that explained the visions.

Unable to sleep, she tossed and turned all night. Were her parents planning to tell her? Probably not. Should she confront her father? Would it change anything? They would still push her into math, and they would load more guilt onto her. It was obvious that if Cora/Catherine lived longer, she could have been a famous mathematician. But that didn't mean Kassie had to be one as well. Cora earned her Ph.D. in a time when woman didn't attend college. She didn't follow the expected path, but pursued her passion.

Kassie sat up in bed. The immense pressure on chest eased with a flash of insight. She hadn't realized how much pressure she was under until the weight was lifted and she was buoyant again.

***

The next day she entered Professor Millen's classroom and marched up to Zeckland and his friends with determination.

"What's wrong, Kass?" Zeckland asked.

The three guys were staring at her in concern.

"I would like you guys to stop copying off me," she said.

Their aura's flashed and sparked for three mouth drying breaths.

"Sure," Levi said.

"No problem," Riley said.

Zeckland remained quiet for a while. Finally, he said, "Sorry, Kass. Still friends?"

"Yes."

"How can I make it up to you?" Zeckland asked.

"Will you go to my senior prom with me?"

Zeckland's purple aura colored toward red. "Senior? As in *high school* senior?"

"Yes. I was afraid to tell you before, but since we're . . . er . . . being honest . . ." Heat flushed up her neck.

"When is it?" he asked.

"May ninth."

Zeckland removed his laptop, typed, and then showed her his updated calendar. "Looking forward to it."

Kassie smiled. At least she had one thing planned for her new future.

***

That night at the dinner table, Kassie upset her mother like a terrorist attack when she announced her decision not to take any additional college-level classes.

"I'm stressed out, can't sleep, and I've had a headache since the first day of school." She cut off her father's outrage at being lied to, "Sorry, Dad, I thought I could handle it, and I didn't want to worry you."

Her father's green aura stayed steady, and Kassie knew he was an ally. Unfortunately, by the nuclear glow coming from her mother, she knew the battle wasn't over.

Before her mother could form a response, Kassie said, "Go ahead and ground me until I'm eighteen, Mom. You can sign me up for college classes, but I won't attend. I'm not changing my mind."

She left the dinner table and returned to her room to finish her research paper for Dr. Millen. Cora was fascinating. When Cora was promoted to full professor, she was one of just four women at Indiana University to hold that rank and a few of her paintings still hang in the university's art gallery.

That night her father came to tuck her into bed.

"Dad, I'm seventeen," she said, trying to sound annoyed.

"Sweets, I don't care how old you are; you're still my little girl."

The truth of his words burned deep down inside her. She always knew she owed her life to him, but that didn't mean she had to live it his way.

He pushed her bangs to the side. "Your mother is having a meltdown, but I explained to her the dangers of putting too much stress on you, and she reluctantly agreed to ease up. What do you want to do now?"

"I want to be a teenager and not some math genius. I want to paint. I want a job."

Her father laughed. "I'll pay you to mow the lawn."

"No. I want to work in the bookstore."

"Why?"

"The colors are amazing. It would be like working in a ninety-six count box of crayons."

"Okay, sweets. Anything for you." He kissed her forehead and pulled the covers up to her chin.

"Dad?" she asked. "If I don't grow up to be a famous mathematician and solve Hilbert's last two problems, will you still love me?" Cora had been working on them before she had died. Of the twenty-three problems he proposed back in 1900, only two remained unsolved.

Ripples shot through his aura, but he maintained his composure. "Of course. I will love you regardless." His voice was weak, and he left her room quickly.

After a few minutes, Kassie hopped out of bed and cracked her door open an inch. Her parents' frantic whispering drifted up from the living room. She smiled. Let them whisper.

Maria V. Snyder *is a* New York Times *best-selling fantasy and science fiction novelist, who has published over a dozen novels and numerous short stories for young adult and adult readers all over the world. Maria enjoys helping other writers and, after earning her Master's degree in Writing from Seton Hill University, she joined their MFA faculty as a mentor and lecturer. Readers are invited to go to her website for more information at http://www.MariaVSnyder.com.*

ON A FULL MOON NIGHT

by Rachel Sink

As soon as the water wicked through my shirt, as soon as the cold fabric clung to my belly, that's when I remembered that life is real and it's once. It's not a book to be closed, reopened, and read all over again. That's what I was trying to do. Close that book and start over again, wishing that this time the ending would be different.

The little boy I left back at the house is real, too—my son, Jordan, alone with red-faced Darrell, who is not his father. My only child, and where was I? Chest-deep in a swampy river, with handfuls of rocks scooped into the sagging pockets of my cardigan, which I had worn because it was the only piece of clothing I owned with pockets that could hold enough weight to get the job done.

I looked over my shoulder toward the riverbank and the house with the yellow-lit windows that deceptively radiated welcome from a distance, the single-glazed, antique glass just barely containing Darrell's tense fury. We had both been drinking, but while alcohol makes me let my guard down, slow and sleepy, it makes Darrell angrily vigilant. When I had left, he was still seething on the couch, staring dead-eyed at the shattered television screen. Jordan was in his bedroom with the door closed, trying not to hear the taut silence that had begun with Darrell and seeped throughout the rest of the house, just after the ring of breaking glass. *Don't look at the goddamn TV; look at* me *when I'm talking to you.*

I had run into my own room and locked the door. Then: the plan, the cardigan, the four-foot drop from the window to the ground, the cracking branches of the azalea under my feet. I was gone—in my mind I was already in a place where Darrell couldn't touch me. But I left an unsolved problem behind. Darrell would provide nothing for Jordan. It would be a miracle if he even bothered to call my mother to come collect her orphan grandchild.

Once, soon after we began dating, Darrell had asked Jordan to fetch him a pack of cigarettes from his car. I had never let anyone smoke inside our house before, and Jordan hesitated and looked at me.

Darrel saw the look. "What are you waiting for, bud?"

His voice was friendly, but his eyes had gone cold.

"It's okay, go on and get them," I'd said. That was the first moment of surrender and, though there would be many others, that was the one I regretted most.

I had allowed Darrell to drive me out of my own house, an invading army of one. His current occupation of the couch would be hazardous for Jordan, who would only be able to last for so long without needing something—some juice, a bedtime story, clean clothes—and Darrell despised need.

I turned and began to wade back toward the house. As I pushed through the sluggish water, it pushed back with leaves, broken twigs, and strands of decaying vegetation. Something solid and rough bumped against me and floated to the side.

The whisper that drifted past my right elbow was so soft that I might have mistaken it for the curtains of Spanish moss rustling in the wind, except that the night was still and muggy. Rather, it might have been the gurgle of swamp gas, the bullfrogs croaking, or my clothing catching on the log I had just brushed against. I adjusted my path to pass by the obstacle, but it slid purposefully through the water to block my way again.

"Not so fast," said the voice, now loud enough to be unmistakable. "Having second thoughts, *chère*?"

Black marble eyes rose out of the dark water, followed by a jagged, reptilian grin.

"When you make a wish on a full moon night, it might just come true, whether you like it or not. Too late to take it back now. I haven't eaten all day, and I'm famished."

I shivered in the warm night air. "You're not real. Logs can't talk and neither can alligators."

"Well, this alligator is talking to you, *chère*, and you'd best listen close because I'm not one to repeat myself."

"I really need to get back to my son. If you let me go, I promise I'll bring you the biggest steak you ever saw in your life."

"A bird in the hand is worth two in the bush," she purred. "But because I am generous of spirit, I'll make you a deal, *chère*. I will take your life, but you can have mine."

"But my son—"

"You don't seem to understand. There's not much choice in the matter. You can be in my skin or in my belly. Skin or belly? Bin or skelly? Bell or skinny?" A rumbling chuckle rolled from her long mouth. "Trust me, *chère*: little Jordan will be the least of your concerns. Surprised? Oh, yes, I know him. He sneaks away sometimes and feeds me marshmallows from the river bank. I've grown fond of him. You'll see I'm quite a devoted mother. Attentive. Protective. Preventive. *Effective*. Shake on it?"

She captured my forearm in her jaws and pressed down with sharp, ivory teeth until I cried, "Okay, yes! Whatever you want, just keep my baby safe."

There was a rush like waves crashing, and I fell backwards, head underwater. I held my breath as I fell and then rose, surfacing slowly, and all at once, stretched in a dead man's float. The swamp no longer felt mucky or clammy. It was as warm as bath water and silty-soft. My body felt hard and tight like a thick rope, a hundred times knotted. I was horrified, the dread made worse by the fact that I could see nothing of myself, except the end of a long, dark tail when it curled behind me. Horrified yet wishing, with an unfamiliar satisfaction, that Darrell could be there to witness my ugly grace and to fear me for once as Jordan and I have feared him for two and a half years.

I peered at the bank through murky eyes, looking for the *her* that was now *me*. She had reached solid ground, as it were, and was pulling herself through the marshy mud. She crawled astonishingly quickly, naked and dripping, with her belly to the ground.

The *her* that was *me* glided to shore and crept along at a distance.

Her skin was moonlit; she was as slick as a pink fish. She passed through the garden, and then, as she neared the house, she seemed to remember the long legs she now owned and drew herself up to full height. She approached the walk where my crystal ball glowed like a second moon. It was only a lawn ornament, a gift from my mother. The pearlescent ball was screwed like a finial onto a long, iron stake planted a foot into the ground. I'd always felt it was too garish and even tacky in daylight, but that night it was striking.

The *her* that was *me* reached down in one smooth motion and heaved the crystal ball out of the ground by its stake. She handlessly whipped her wet hair over her shoulder and proceeded up the porch steps. She lifted her bare foot and kicked it in the front door—a solid, live oak slab—as casually as I would have pushed through a dressing room curtain.

From inside came an explosion of yelling, snarling, and the sound of unbreakable things being broken. Darrell tore through the splintered doorway in nothing but boxer shorts and a coat of cold sweat. He went for the pickup truck, but she was somehow already a step ahead of him. She was wielding the sharpened end of the iron stake, still caked with soil, and swinging it at Darrell's head. It whistled through the air as he jumped back just in time.

She laughed as he flinched. "Don't even think of taking my truck."

"What's the matter with you, Jeanette? How am I supposed to leave if I can't take the truck?"

His voice sounded so clear and alert that if I didn't know better I would have thought he was sober. But the new Jeanette was in no mood to talk; she answered by swinging the stake so hard that the crystal ball flew off, hurtled past Darrell's head, and smashed against the side of the house.

"Jeanette, will you just listen to me?" he pleaded. "We're miles from anywhere."

"Best get to walking, then," she growled, finally clipping him with the stake.

He squealed like a stuck pig and clapped his hand across his already bleeding shoulder. Then, after one final, disbelieving stare, he lit out across the front yard and down the lane, yelling obscenities behind him.

The *her* that was *me* threw her head back and cackled. She turned and went inside.

I thought about spending the night in the crawl space under the house. I could creep right under Jordan's bed and sleep there, just to make sure he was safe. But an alligator under the house is a bad omen. It means someone's going to die. I decided to go back to the swamp. As I shuffled through the long grass, I whispered prayers and fought back tears that I wasn't sure would come.

I pushed off the bank into the water and let myself float like a log on the surface, effortless. Just as I was drifting off, I heard voices coming from the house. It was her, and she had Jordan with her. When they came into view I saw that she had dressed herself in my terrycloth robe, the sash awkwardly knotted. She led Jordan toward the swamp, toward me. She held a flashlight in one hand and her other hand was around Jordan's shoulder. Jordan held a bag that looked as if it was full of cotton.

When they reached the muddy bank, she swept the flashlight back and forth until the beam hit me straight in the eyes. I hissed involuntarily and sank deeper into the dark water.

"There she is!" Jordan pointed and danced closer to the water.

She grabbed him by the shirt collar. "Not too close, *chère.* Never too close."

They knelt down and Jordan struggled to open the bag.

"Mama," he said, handing it to her to open, "what if Darrell comes back?"

"He won't," she said with a wide grin. "He best not, or I'll eat him up!"

Her fearless laughter rang out like a bell in the night, an invitation for Darrell to come back and tangle if he dared. Jordan's face relaxed and he giggled, delighted with his fierce new mama.

Something plopped into the swamp beside me. I could feel the water level creeping up and down, up and down, against my open eyes. Without thinking, I followed the ripple to its center, where a white thing was suspended in the cloudy water. It was a marshmallow.

"Mama, she's not eating it. She's not hungry."

"Gators is always hungry, *chère*," she murmured.

And I found that I was. I opened my jaws and let the marshmallow float into my mouth. It tasted earthy and swampy and sweet.

Rachel Sink *lives in Harrisburg, PA with her husband, daughter, and plenty of critters to keep things lively. Her favorite hobbies are art, gardening, and both reading and writing fiction. She has self-published an e-book collection of three short stories called* God's Country *and is currently working on a novel-length piece. She enjoys writing about extraordinary moments or experiences that occur within ordinary lives.*

THE DRAGON'S EYE

(In the Way of Fairy Tales)

by Samantha Coons

Once upon a time in a small village there lived a man and a woman who ran a farm by the deep forest. The farmers had a small daughter, and the three of them were very happy together. The girl grew up tall and bright, and was a great help to her parents, who were always very proud. Unfortunately, when the girl reached a certain age, her mother fell ill after working in the rain, and passed soon after. Before she died, the girl's mother pressed her pair of hide gloves, an old rough handkerchief, and a tarnished compass into the girl's hands. She told her daughter that she had seen they would bring her luck, as they had once brought her luck. The girl had no time to wonder about her mother's words as she was soon grieving with her father.

A few years passed. The girl tended the farm with as much care as her parents had, but her father took to spending longer and longer nights at the village inn. He would drink with the blacksmith and the tanner and the mayor, who would sit and talk with him for hours. The tanner and the mayor were good enough men and did their best to ease the farmer's heart over the loss of his wife and the future of his daughter. But the blacksmith was cruel and crafty, and the girl had caught his eye.

"Your daughter seems like a clever little thing," he said one night, after the tanner and the mayor had left for the evening.

The farmer smiled into his drink.

"She is, bless her. Not sure what I'd do without her around."

"Still," the blacksmith said, his brow wrinkled, "seems a shame for such a clever girl to be stuck farming the rest of her life."

The farmer's smile was gone as he took a long drink.

"She's about the age to go out and make her way in the world, isn't she? Hell, I think most folks would be happy to take her in as an apprentice." The blacksmith watched the farmer as he spoke. "A girl like that . . . why, I bet your next drink that she could bring in your whole harvest by herself."

The farmer chuckled and took a long swig of beer.

"I wouldn't bet against you there. I would bet my best axe that she could take over the whole farm tomorrow if she wanted."

The blacksmith laughed and slapped the farmer on the back. The two continued making more and more ridiculous bets on behalf of the farmer's daughter, each time nodding along.

"Become mayor? Child's play."

"Marry the prince? Easy as a dream."

"Defeat the king in combat? In her sleep!"

By now the farmer was leaning heavily on the bar, surrounded by empty glasses.

"I bet . . ." the farmer started, pausing as he swayed in his chair. "I bet *her hand in marriage* that she could defeat the one and only Iron Dragon!"

The blacksmith grinned.

***

The girl's father stayed out talking to the blacksmith until dawn spread across the fields. He and the sunlight arrived home together. The girl started as the door opened with a creak. She had been sitting by the fire waiting for her father's return and had nodded off. She took his arm and led him to bed. He mumbled something as she tucked a blanket around him but was soon fast asleep. The girl did not think twice about it as she went about her chores on the farm.

When she returned to make breakfast, her father was sitting at the table with his head in his hands.

"Father?"

Her father let out a long sigh and told her to sit down. "Forgive your fool of a father." He grasped her hands as he told her, tears running down his cheeks. But she simply listened, her eyes steady. He told her that the night before he had been tricked into an agreement with the blacksmith. She would have to either leave her home and defeat the Iron Dragon, or he would be forced to hand her over in marriage to the blacksmith. The barman had witnessed the agreement. It was final.

When he finished, she gently released his hands and went into her room. The farmer wept, swearing never to drink again. "I will go to the mayor today!" he called out to her. "I will go to the king if I must. Fool that I am. I shall never drink again!"

To his surprise, his daughter came back out, a heavy cloak on her shoulders and a rucksack on her back.

"I will return within half a year," she told her father. She gave him a kiss on the forehead and walked out the door.

***

She ventured North, carrying only food and water and the few keepsakes her mother had given her. The girl walked through the night (sleeping only a few hours at dawn), and through the rain and wind. She walked until all she had left to eat was a thin loaf of brown bread, an apple, and a drop of water in her water skein.

The sound of burbling water brought her off the path into a small grove. She stooped to fill her water skein at the small, cheerful spring, and as she straightened she noticed an old, withered willow amongst the lush, green pines.

"Poor willow. You look even more desperate for a drink than I am."

She sprinkled fresh water over its cracked, upturned roots. The roots eagerly soaked up the water. She gave the willow a satisfied smile and turned to refill her skein. As she turned back to the willow, an old brown woman with long knotted hair stepped out from the green pines. The girl's eyes widened.

"Young traveler, thank you for your kindness to this old woman. I had forgotten myself, forgotten by Mother Rain, Father Sun, and by all those who passed me. Your water has brought me back. Please, tell me—Mother Greenwillow—what I can do to help."

The old woman's smile calmed the girl. She was no stranger to the tales of the woodland spirits and knew that as she had done a good turn, so would Mother Greenwillow do for her.

"Mother Greenwillow, I am going North to defeat the Iron Dragon, so that I may have a life of my own. I fear it is something that I must do alone."

Mother Greenwillow patted her hand as she took her water skein, bending to refill it.

"Young traveler, it is lucky that you came to me. You must be very careful as you continue on your journey, North. You will come to a mountain made entirely of silver—Mount Chisai. Offer the silver guardian of Chisai your bread before she speaks and do as she bids. Then, you will come to a mountain made of gold—Mount Heikin. Offer the golden guardian your apple and do as she bids. Finally you will reach Mount O, which is a great diamond mountain. Offer the guardian of Mount O this skein of water and do as she bids. If you do as I say, you will reach the dragon. You must trust yourself."

She handed the girl her water skein, and pressed a small sack smelling of water lilies into her hand.

"This is sap from my tree. If you are injured, only spread a little on the wound, and it will heal."

The girl thanked Mother Greenwillow and promised she would stop at the spring on her way home.

She continued North, thinking over Mother Greenwillow's words. She had not walked a full day before coming to the base of a mountain. She blinked and then gasped as the sun shone on the face of Mount Chisai, beaming silver light onto the path

A woman cloaked in silver fox fur perched at the tunnel's entrance. The girl ran forward with her brown bread and offered it to the woman.

"You are very kind," the woman said. The girl watched in silence as she slowly ate.

After she had finished the girl asked, "May I pass through the tunnel?"

The woman looked at her with a blank face.

"To pass you must sacrifice your beauty."

The girl thought about this but could not riddle out what the woman meant.

"How?" she asked.

"A piece of your hair will do."

The girl, relieved, happily plucked a few strands of her hair and handed them to the guardian. The woman dropped the hairs at the tunnel's entrance. The hairs twisted and flamed and as they burned, the girl felt a flash of heat through her scalp. The guardian stepped aside and waved the girl onward.

The tunnel was dark, and as she reached out to feel her way along the tunnel's walls, she yelped. "Ouch! They're sharp." The girl dug out her mother's gloves and slid them on. She felt her way along, her hands protected under the thick leather.

After what seemed like hours, she finally came to a sunlit path up ahead! She paused, and caught her reflection in the silver, mirror-like walls. Her skin sagged, her coarse hair was charred. She bit her lip, sighed, and skipped ahead into the full sun. Outside, the gloves crumbled and floated like ash to her feet.

She continued on the path, and before long, Mount Heikin appeared as suddenly as the silver mountain had. A woman sat at the foot of the mountain robed in a golden lion skin cloak. The girl withdrew her apple. She held it out to the woman, who accepted it with a nod.

"It is rare for us to receive a gift."

After the woman had eaten the apple down to the core, the girl asked if she could pass.

"You must sacrifice a part of your being."

Although this sounded even more alarming than sacrificing her beauty, she asked, "How?"

The woman smiled wide, and the girl saw that all her teeth were sharp points.

"A little blood will do. Give me your hand."

Remembering how simple the last guardian's odd request had been to fulfill, the girl did not hesitate to hold out her arm.

The guardian caught her wrist tight, and bit into her fingertip. She turned to the tunnel's entrance and spit the girl's blood on the ground, where it sizzled.

The girl felt heat travel up her arms, and she shrieked. The pain died to a tingle, and she reached into her sack to smear Mother Greenwillow's sap on her finger, which healed instantly. The guardian stepped aside, waving the girl into the tunnel.

The tunnel's path twisted and turned. When she came to a fork, she brought out her mother's compass, and followed the arrow faithfully. As she stumbled out into the sun again, she tripped and dropped the compass. It fell and was swallowed into the mountain's golden crevices. The girl's heart sank at another loss of her mother's keepsakes.

She continued her trek, and eventually reached Mount O. A woman draped in a shimmery white bear skin stood before her. The girl handed her water to the diamond woman, who drained it in the blink of an eye.

"May I pass into the mountain?" the girl asked.

"You must sacrifice a piece of your sense before you can pass."

"What can I give?"

The woman gave her a long look.

"One of your eyes."

The girl took a step back, and reached up to touch her eye. She wanted to finish her quest, but she didn't know if the woman really meant what she said.

The woman approached, her own bright eyes calm.

"Do you want me to do it?"

The girl nodded. Surely this business of removing an eye sounded worse than it would actually be.

The girl stood as still as she could, her heart pounding. The woman cupped her hand over the girl's eye and pulled. There was a tight tugging sensation, and then the girl blinked, and half of the world was gone. But there was no pain.

The woman dropped her eye at the tunnel's entrance, where it twisted and flamed as the other sacrifices had. The girl's stomach dropped when the guardian lead her by the hand toward the tunnel.

"Luck to you, young traveler," she said as the girl stepped into the diamond mountain's tunnel.

The warm twinkling light enveloped her as she felt her way through the tunnel. Tears streamed from her eye, and she withdrew her mother's handkerchief to wipe her face.

It wasn't long before she came upon the tunnel's exit. She stepped into the sun, and the handkerchief slipped from her hand. Where it fell, she could not see. But the last tunnel was now behind her, and for that reason, she knelt and thanked her mother three times for watching over her. And although it was dusk and she could hardly see, she continued on her way.

She felt the last rays of the sun on her back as she smacked into something hard and cold. It was a wall, of sorts, and it blocked her path. She felt up and down the surface with her hands. Short ledges jutted out, like handles, and she grasped them, considering her options. Climb this wall, or try to walk around it? She knew better than to stray from the path, so she made sure her rucksack was secure and started climbing. The rough and uneven wall was easy to scale, and she made it to the top with little effort. She swung her legs over and dropped to the ground.

She heaved herself to her feet, and took a few careful steps. Something didn't seem right.

There was movement ahead. The girl ambled her way toward the heavy breathing.

"If you're here to slay me, you might as well get it over with."

She started at the reedy voice. Sunken, beady eyes glared at her.

The dragon? It seemed . . . small. Sure enough the beast wasn't even as big as the horses on the farm.

"Are you . . . are you the Iron Dragon?"

It snorted and a puff of flame shot from its snout. "That's what they tell me. Are you here to slay me?"

The girl nodded and fidgeted with the clasp on her pack.

"Like I said, get it over with."

The girl thought about reaching into her rucksack, but for what? What did she have to slay the dragon with? She had thought she might find a weapon along her way, and hadn't bothered to bring one. She had contemplated death, knowing a weapon would be useless against a mighty beast. But this poor animal looked thin. Even as weak as she was, she doubted she would have trouble ending its life.

She sat down and tucked her legs under her.

"How did you get here?" she asked.

The dragon's eyes narrowed as he focused on her eye socket.

"A long time ago, my older sister killed a human king and tore down his castle . . . the last of the knights caught me and handed me over to a warlock who tied me upon this hill top."

The dragon huffed and then looked away.

For the first time, she noticed a thick bloody rope around the dragon's neck. She reached out and ran her fingers over the fibers—the rope was cold, despite the heat radiating from the dragon's chest.

"Would I be able to cut through it?" she asked.

The dragon rolled its shoulders in a shrug.

"I haven't been able to do any damage with my claws. But if you want to try." It shrugged again.

The girl grabbed her rucksack and started rummaging, but the only thing left was Mother Greenwillow's sap. She opened the bowl and stared into the thick liquid. She scooped the sap onto her fingers and smeared it along the dragon's bloody wound.

To her surprise, the rope began melting away.

The dragon stared at the fallen rope for a long time. Then it swung back its head and roared, its wings stretching out as it jumped into the air. It beat its wings and flew around the field, fire trailing from its mouth as it roared its freedom.

The girl watched from her place on the ground, a small smile lighting up her face.

After a few more rounds, the dragon landed beside the girl.

"My friend," the dragon said, "Thank you. I am . . . I can finally . . . my family."

Tears filled the dragon's eyes. The girl placed her hand on the dragon's snout. Its eyes shut and the thin shoulders began to tremble.

"I was happy to help," the girl said.

"Thank you. Tell me, please, is there anything I can do for you?"

The girl's smile faded.

She wrapped her arms around his scaled neck and told him everything that had happened to her. It listened quietly.

"Then you only need a token to prove you have succeeded."

The girl released the dragon and stepped back.

"But I haven't defeated you. It wouldn't be fair."

The dragon shook out its wings.

"I was the Iron Dragon when I was tethered. Now I am only me. So you did defeat the Iron Dragon." The dragon reached up and scooped out its left eye, holding it out to her. "I think this should prove your deed. Don't worry, it doesn't hurt. Dragons have our own magic you know."

Mouth agape, she reached out to take the eye. The dragon nodded, brought the eye to her face, and slid it into her empty socket.

Her sight returned, the world vivid. Her muscles felt stronger. She jumped and whooped, and wondered giddily if she could fly.

"Thank you!" she shouted.

The dragon smiled, its scaly cheeks dimpling. "Would you like a ride back home?"

She sighed. "Oh, yes. Take me over the mountains, to the pine trees by the babbling stream. There's someone else I need to see first."

The girl climbed aboard her new friend. The dragon beat its wings and was up in the air in an instant, soaring high.

In what seemed like no time at all, she was at Mother Greenwillow's tree. "I can find my way from here," she said. The girl gave the dragon one last hug, and the two parted. She greeted Mother Greenwillow, who listened to her story and nodded, saying it was well what she had done. Then the girl went on her way with Mother Greenwillow's luck in her ears.

It was dusk when she arrived into town. She headed straight to the tavern, where, despite his promise, she knew she would find her father and the blacksmith. When she entered, everyone stilled and stared. Her hair was tangled and caught into a knot on her head, her clothes torn and dirty, and her eyes . . . one ordinary, one bright golden with a slit pupil. While the others looked on in horror, her father's eyes widened, and his hands shook as he pulled himself out of his chair. She barely had time to smile as he ran over and crushed her in his arms with a great hug.

She patted his back and sniffed, tears welling in her eyes.

"I'm okay," she whispered. "I'm fine."

He drew back and beamed at her. "You are your mother's daughter," he said.

"I've won the bet," she said, holding her head high.

The blacksmith stared from across the bar. He seemed to about to say something, then cowered, drawing into himself.

She turned back to her father; his smile was glued to his face.

"Let's go home," he said. He slapped some money on the table. "Last round is on me, fellas." The other men in the tavern, most still scratching their heads in bewilderment, cheered and slapped the farmer and the girl on the back as they left.

***

Over the next few days the girl told her father everything that had happened. When she finished, he said, "You mean to go find the dragon then."

She nodded.

Despite her father's urging, she stayed in his house only a month longer, making sure everything was well in order. Then she put on her cloak and rucksack once again, and headed South.

Samantha Coon's *first story was written before she could write (her father transcribed it). Her head has always been in the clouds, and that's the way she likes it.*

HAUNTING IN SHIPOKE

by Lori M. Myers

Ghost's sanctuary lay inside a corner of a magazine photo of a woman. He nestled alongside the auburn sheen of her hair, the furrows of her brow, her tight smile. Victor, who'd lived in this ten-room farmhouse years before with his mother, had tacked the color page onto a rear bedroom wall for Ghost. Ghost truly believed that Victor, an odd-sort dressed in buttoned-up clothes, who walked crooked and had an angular haircut, wanted Ghost to feel safe; had created a place for him to burrow and contemplate his past as human and his present and future as a wisp of smoke, spinning in slow motion. Every few months after he moved out, Victor visited the new residents, asked if everything was okay, and searched for Ghost who'd tug at his shirt as a sign. After Victor's mother died (Ghost overheard the husband telling the wife), Victor stopped visiting. Ghost clung inside the woman's hairline, listening to the home's residents' comings and goings, hoping to see Victor again.

Whenever Ghost was sure the family was out of the house, he'd slip out of the photo and wander in and around the empty rooms, sometimes soaring into the library where he'd spend hours gazing at the smooth hard cover volumes by Aquinas and Spinoza. Other times he floated from the kitchen, with its lingering aroma of toast and coffee, into the living room where he bounced on the floral sofa then up to the pink bedroom where the child slept, until he finally drifted upstairs to nestle once again inside the glossy page tacked onto a crumbling plaster wall. Every so often, he'd chance settling on the arm of the child as she romped and tumbled. It was safe to do so; she called it dust, and he never let on otherwise.

One night, as a thick fog blanketed the valley, Leon and Phillip of the undead, and Sabra who was much like Ghost, appeared on the doorstep. Leon and Phillip reeked of rotted flesh and their lips were stained with days' old blood. They wanted him, missed him they claimed, and urged him to return to Shipoke graveyard where they'd befriended others of their kind, haunting the vine-choked tombs. There the crickets chirped and bats swooped as close to the ground as they dared. The cemetery's ghouls delighted in the terror they caused young lovers and bag ladies who wandered through.

"We need you," Leon said to Ghost at the threshold. "You think you're still of human form, but you're far from it."

"Ghost, you're in denial," Phillip said, his tongue lapping the air.

Sabra batted her eyelashes, her eyes round and dreamy. "Come back," was all she said. Her voice decibeled above a whisper, a dangerous rattle echoing in her throat.

Ghost had spent years searching for escape from Shipoke, the prison-of-a-graveyard, where the ghouls emerged only after the moon shone above the hilltops. He didn't want to leave this home despite it being odd to be living with humans, whose veins teemed with fresh blood, and who smelled like roses, their skin soft as petals. Ghost figured he smelled and felt like nothing at all but preferred his heart beating among the living, not the undead.

"There's freedom here, even curled up in the woman's photo," Ghost said as he floated above the tiled foyer, ready to take off if the trio made a sudden move.

But it was too late.

Leon and Phillip grabbed Ghost around his middle as Sabra leaned against the door, holding it open. The three rushed out and into the rusted jalopy. Leon's coarse cheek scratched Ghost, and his foul breath made Ghost nauseous. Sabra settled into the truck bed next to piles of rags and animal carcasses and, as the jalopy made its way toward Route 59, air feathered through her like a tickle.

The sliver of moon barely lit the dirt driveway and the warm moist darkness muffled Ghost's screams. Phillip sat on top of Ghost and held him solid to the seat, blocking his forward view. All he could see were Leon's bony fingers gripping the steering wheel, and his red-rimmed eyes almost neon, with a light in them, an excitement that the moon's sliver was unable to electrify. It was the "taking" tonight that had sparked his hunger and desires. He opened the driver's side window half way and turned up the volume on the radio. It crackled and halted until some punk tune proclaimed "Gonna have me some fun tonight/It's gonna make it all right, all right, all right/Yeah, man, some fun tonight."

"Now we're complete," Leon snorted, jerking his body like a frenzied worm. He leaned out the window, a breeze mussing his fringe of hair at the nape of his neck, and made up his own words to the song. Something about sun, and fright. And that's when Ghost knew that this was more than a kidnapping.

Ghost could feel Phillip's weight, smell his decay, his sharp bones digging like knives into Ghost's smoky haunches. He lost track of time, and it seemed like they were driving around in circles.

"There's the liquor store," Leon said smacking his lips. "Been a long time. I need a drink."

Ghost knew that neither Leon nor Phillip had touched liquor in at least fifty or sixty years, maybe longer, so it was unlikely it was beer or pinot they were after. Leon parked the jalopy perpendicular to the sidewalk, blocking another car from getting out of the space should the driver arrive.

"All right," Leon said as he shut off the truck. "We'll need you inside, Ghost."

Leon wandered to the back of the dilapidated store where the cheap liquor was shelved. Phillip clutched Ghost and kept a tight grip, his razor-sharp nails gouging into Ghost's transparency. Even in ghost form, pain shot through him. Sabra stood sentry at the door. Every so often, she picked up several of the small bottles of vodka piled up in a display and flung them across the room much to the amazement of the young clerk who gaped at the airborne bottles that appeared to soar on their own. His wide eyes moved side to side, back and forth—from Leon to Phillip and back again, as if at a tennis match.

Ghost noticed the sparkle in Leon's eyes as he returned to the front of the store, clutching the neck of what looked like cheap whiskey. Leon's nostrils flared as he sniffed the young man. Smelling meat, he circled the clerk who stood frozen near the front door (and, unbeknownst to him, next to Sabra, who was caressing his ankle with her foot.) The clerk's body stiffened, his jaw bones growing so rigid it looked like his face would break.

"That's okay, sir," he said to Leon. "Just take it. A gift."

"Hey, man, that's sweet of ya," Leon said as he scrutinized the young man from every angle as if he were a porterhouse in a supermarket's meat section. "But if I don't hafta pay, then you do for your scrumptiousness."

He twisted the bottle cap and guzzled a generous swig, his protruding Adam's apple bobbing up and down inside his emaciated neck. "Mmm. Warms me up. But no one can live on liquor alone, although some do try." He grinned, his few teeth were yellowed and chipped.

"Just go. No . . . Pay." For several seconds, puberty became a stranger as the young man's voice went high soprano. Sweat flowed from his neatly trimmed sideburns, and he made no move to wipe it away as it dripped onto the stiff collar of his pink Oxford shirt. Phillip mumbled under his breath, his patience with Leon wearing thin.

Then Ghost thought that perhaps he could squeeze out of Phillip's vise, but he didn't want to get trapped in this small space with three beings after him. "Cut it out, Leon. Let's go and get Ghost back where he belongs."

Leon ignored Phillip's demand. He continued to dissect the clerk with his eyes, imagined the juicy gorged innards, the virginal flavor that came only from the young and untainted.

If he knew what Leon was capable of, Ghost thought, *this young man would regret his own goodness for it is that goodness for which the animals yearn.*

Just at that moment there was a screech of metal on metal, a sickening quiet, then the squeal of tires. Leon twisted his head in the direction of the commotion as a car whizzed by, its broken bumper creating sparks as it scraped the macadam.

"What the . . .?" Leon's gnarled hands formed fists, and he hurled the bottle in the clerk's direction, missing his head by inches. "Looks like that asshole smashed the side of the truck. Let's get outta here and get 'em."

Phillip gave an audible sigh and dragged Ghost outside behind Leon and Sabra. There was a large dent on the passenger door and side of the cab, and the side view mirror had been knocked off and left shattered on the ground. In the frenzy, the driver's car had turned the jalopy around so it faced in the opposite direction. They all piled into the truck's cab as Leon slammed his foot on the gas and ripped through town.

"There he is!" Leon said as he veered almost out of control. The culprit's car, a crimson Ford, raced ahead, swerving in a dance with the jalopy. Ghost tried to slither in-between Leon and Sabra on the seat for a better view but would end up heaped on the floor every time Leon jammed the brakes. Soon Leon overtook the Ford and blocked it between a graffitied wall of splintered wood and a streetlight.

"Grab Ghost," Leon commanded. "He needs to see what'll happen if he doesn't cooperate."

Phillip did as he was told, and they watched as a middle-aged man, his long-sleeved white shirt buttoned up to his neck, climbed out of the Ford and stared back at them, his body trembling, his back against the wall in an effort to be as far away as possible from Leon's yellowed eyes and trail of drool. The man's crooked walk was as angular as his hair, peppered with white and grey. A wet spot soiled the front of his khakis.

Victor.

Ghost tried to wiggle out of Phillip's clutches, but he held firm digging deeply into Ghost's smoldering mass. Phillip's tongue jutted out as he sniffed the night's aroma, his eyes wide and wild, bulging. Blood. Flesh. He could taste it, bathe in it. Pure. Ghost knew the signs of thirst in the undead after years of joining them in graveyard jaunts and haunts. Victor, forever single, untouched, a momma's boy; the ultimate seduction to others such as Leon and Phillip who craved such temptation. Ghost wanted to tug Victor's shirt, give him a sign, save him.

"Forget it," Leon shouted, noticing Phillip's hunger. "He's mine!"

Phillip spiraled his head in Leon's direction; his exposed bones wet with sweat. He shook like an earth's tremor and tossed Ghost to the side of the road. Sabra rushed to Ghost, her own smoke breaking up into tiny shadows.

"Come with me," she urged, reaching out a hazy appendage.

Ghost almost took it. Almost. He could escape, perhaps with Sabra if she was willing. If not, he would find his way home, to the photo of the woman with the teased hair tacked onto plaster and tuck back, in a tiny corner of her hairline; return to roaming the rooms of the house as a wisp of smoke, riding the tender arm of the young child who knew him as "dust."

"Ghost, stop you're dreaming." It was Sabra again, alerting him. "You know this won't end well. Poor man. Let's return to the graveyard ahead of them. Let them have their fun and their dinner. They're disgusting. We know."

"I can't." Even Ghost couldn't believe his own words. Here was his chance for freedom from Phillip's bony limbs encircling him in a smother-hold; from Leon's foul breath and crazed behavior.

Something inside restrained Ghost as he watched Leon and Phillip snarl at each other and then start to descend upon Victor who hugged the wall, his body contorted, stiff. They were several yards away when lightning flashed in the sky and swirls of leaves and papers gathered like tumbleweeds around them. The streetlight flickered; the wind whooshed and water fell in torrents. Leon and Phillip ceased stalking their prey as the drops pinpricked their disintegrating skin.

Ghost shivered as the rain cut through him. He would disappear if he didn't seek shelter soon; it was even difficult to decipher Sabra's form at this point. He looked into Victor's face and felt his heart beating. He looked into Leon's face and saw evil, without conscience, yearning to satisfy its appetite. Nature must have seen it too. It responded with a good soaking rain

Victor, the untainted, the good, also recognized the evil before him. He stared, wide-eyed and pleading, at Ghost.

He can see me. He knows who I am, Ghost thought.

Ghost squirmed away from Sabra's grasp, rushed toward Victor and enveloped him with his translucency. The rain slowed as Leon and Phillip came to their senses, grunted at each other, and realized what they were in the process of doing. They dived into Victor, shunting Ghost aside to reach their prey, sinking their jaws into either side of Victor's neck, puncturing and gnawing at his intestines. They both took turns cursing and growling at each other as they nourished themselves. Victor groaned, his tears causing more of Ghost to erode.

"Help me, Ghost," he cried, his body splayed on the macadam. Blood and body parts fell in pools around him.

A shattered Ghost struggled and kicked, but Leon and Phillip's hunger and determination proved the heaviest of weights. Victor lay open and splattered on the ground. There was silence, except for the satisfied chomp-chomp and smacking of lips of the feasters. There were gurgling sounds, too, as blood surged down the undeads' throats.

Nourished and sated, Leon and Phillip carried Ghost and Sabra to Shipoke graveyard, carefully placing their pieces onto the jalopy seat between them and driving away as the sliver of moon disappeared beyond the cardboard box houses of the town's lost and homeless.

***

The cemetery was as Ghost remembered: overgrown berberis and blackthorns—Prunus spinosa, with spines and prickles that bloodied daring visitors' fingers and legs. Masses of Hedera and devil's ivy choked the place. Grimy, cracked headstones stood rigid against the next; a picket fence lay in the mud.

Ghost tried to settle into the once familiar surrounding. Pieces of him held on by a whisper, and he dared not move too quickly lest he lose parts of his spirit-being.

The seasons changed. He became more whole but grew tired of frightening trespassers. One hot summer night, He heard the bushes rustle and he looked toward the lights of the town. Out of the shadows, a contorted outline limped onto the graveyard, his buttoned-up shirt now flowed in tatters around his devoured cadaver, his neck gashed, an arm missing, an eye socket hollow.

"Ghost," he whispered. A breeze grazed his angular hair.

He placed his bony fingers into his pocket, removed a folded piece of paper, and opened it for Ghost to see. Ghost could barely make out the contents in the man's trembling hand. As he adjusted his vision in the near darkness, he recognized the photo from a magazine. Unmistakable. A pale-faced woman with auburn hair, furrowed brow, tight smile. Ghost inhaled, circled his smoke as an orb, and rested atop the woman's head as Victor tacked the page into a cracked headstone.

Lori M. Myers *is an award-winning writer of creative nonfiction, fiction, essays and plays, as well as a Pushcart Prize and Broadway World nominee. Lori writes for* TheBurg *magazine in Harrisburg, and other publications. She is the author of* Crawlspace, *a short story collection of dark fiction and horror.*

THE LOLIPOP ANGEL

Excerpt from ALWAYS HERE

by Brenda Jadych

June went into the pet store to pick up her paycheck, which was delayed for everyone this week due to technical difficulty. Bella walked into the pet store with her mom, who worked there as assistant manager. Bella noticed the feisty cocker spaniel behind the glass partition that let shoppers see inside to the grooming area. The little dog wanted to lick every finger and face instead of sit still and be pampered.

"That's Minska's dog. You can sit with her while I go pick up my paycheck." Bella's mom motioned to a bench near the grooming window.

The woman sitting on the bench wore a long red dress that came to points at the bottom, and a plastic red hair band covered with rhinestones that sparkled from the lights when she moved her head.

"It's okay—she knows me," her mom said, nudging her to go over and have a seat.

Minska was watching her dog play with the groomers. "She's so bad," she said out loud to herself. Bella climbed onto the bench and peered through the window from a kneeling position.

"Is that your dog?" she asked Minska. "She's funny."

"Yes, that's my bad dog. She never behaves." They both giggled, watching the two groomers trying to get the dog situated. Bella liked how the woman pronounced *that* as *dat.*

"My mommy said she knows you."

"You're June's daughter? Oh, I hear all about you!"

A proud smile spread from cheek to cheek on Bella.

"I know you like to go to the park, and—" she held out a closed fist and rolled her wrist palm-side up, "I know your favorite is grape!" She opened her palm, and a flurry of twinkling red pixie dust the color of her dress formed a purple lollipop. Bella's mouth opened in surprise.

"How did you do that?"

"I didn't," the woman said, watching the groomers brush her now-settled bad dog.

"Who did?" Bella smiled. Minska was probably teasing her, and Bella wanted to play along.

"The Lollipop Angel, of course."

"There's no such thing," Bella contested, not sure if the woman was joking because she kept a straight face.

"What? Then, who is it that lives beside the Tooth Fairy?" Minska folded her arms across her chest, leaving her long red fingernails exposed, and one index finger tapping against her arm. Her eyebrows raised in a playful challenge.

Unable to come up with an answer, Bella was stumped into submission and shrugged her shoulders. "I thought angels were up in heaven?" she continued, confused.

"There are many angels in heaven," Minska confirmed, "but there are also angels all around. Do you know that every person has their own guardian angel? You have one, I have one, and that man over there, and your mommy." She had Bella's full attention.

"Can I talk to them?" Bella asked, excited to do so.

"We can't see them, but they're around us," Minska nodded affirmatively. "And they only have one job, and that is to protect us. They never leave our side as long as we live." She continued the angel lesson. "For example, if somebody fell on the steps and hurt their knee," she tapped Bella's leg, "the guardian angel makes sure you only need a band-aid, and that you don't break your whole leg." Bella studied the lollipop, turning it around, looking for a secret message about the tumble down the hallway steps she took yesterday when she was running.

"The difference between the guardian angels and the angels in heaven is that the guardian angel is always here, but the other angels can only come down if we ask them."

"Why?" asked a bewildered Bella.

"They're not allowed to just come down and fix everything. Sometimes, we have to learn a lesson. So if somebody fell on the steps and they cry, 'Oh, this hurts,' the angels hear," she pulled at her own ear, "but they're in heaven going like this." She put her chin in her hand and imitated being bored. 'I hear you, but you don't ask for help yet so I cannot come down and help you.' That way, maybe the person will learn the lesson not to run on the steps."

Bella's mom came over to the bench and greeted Minska. Bella held up her treat for her mom to see.

"Did you say thank you?"

"Thank you," Bella told Minska. She inched her way off the bench, realizing that her long pants hid the pink and white Dora the Explorer band-aid on her knee. She turned back to Minska. "How did you know I fell on the steps?"

"The Lollipop Angel told me," she replied with a wink.

Brenda Tadych *is a Pennsylvania native and a graduate of Harrisburg Area Community College. She was a participant in the charter PCCA* A Novel Idea *Writing Workshop. She gave birth to her first "serious" writing, which was published as a letter to the editor, while on hold for one and one-half infuriating hours with the unemployment office. She has freelanced ever since, and has been a contributing writer since 2011 for the Dauphin County publication* Woman, *and has been published in the* Hummelstown Sun, The Patriot-News, *and Wisdom-Magazine.com.*

THE BLACK DRESS

by Donna Leiss

The woman stares at the black dress hanging on the closet door. She recognizes the garment for what it is—her widow's dress. This is the dress she will wear to her husband's funeral.

The garment swallows up her slight frame as she slips it over her head. Even so, it feels constrictive as if trying on a new leather glove. The suffocating feeling dissipates as she zips it up and moves to the bureau's mirror. At first glance, the dress is simple like the first months of their marriage. Her eyes hone in on their wedding picture on the dresser. Captured forever, her fairy tale come true . . . humble girl marries the most sought after bachelor. Everyone questioned how she got so lucky, even herself.

She smiles feeling the softness of the sheath against her skin. It's like his touch on their wedding day. Like her face in the picture, supple and luminous. So much love in her eyes gazing at the smile on her husband's face. How her legs melted and her breath hitched the first time she came face to face with that beaming grin.

Scowling, she smoothes down the black dress's sheer overlay. A mere five months was all it took to see through her husband's charming façade. A darkness crossed him as he pushed her face first into the wall and slammed himself into her over and again. He grunted while she could barely breathe, afraid to. He left her to puddle onto the floor in shock, while he sauntered away whistling. She got to her feet and wiped away tears of shame. Her mother's advice - wives should be seen and never heard, especially in regard to her husband's proclivities.

She learned not to discuss their matters with others, not even her pregnancy. She prepared a candlelight dinner for the announcement, ruined by his late arrival. Her husband flew into a rage at the news. The verbal abuse and accusations worse than the beating she endured. Her knees buckling at the rest of the memory—him dragging her out of the house to a so-called doctor who violated her. The abortion underway before she could comprehend what was happening.

Snatching the dress's corded sash, she ties it tight around her tiny waist. He made it clear they were never going to have babies. They made wives fat and took time away from their husbands, and he would not have either. The belt, made of woven silk threads, reminiscent of umbilical cords of children she would never have. Her womb, like the tasseled ends of the belt, hung lifelessly.

She shakes her head putting the memory back into the deep recesses of her mind where reality blurs and disappears altogether. Skeletal fingers move to the neckline of black beads and crystals. The accessories, dainty at both shoulders graduating into large enhancements set below her thin neck. Fragile body like a bird. Keeping her in his stifling cage wasn't enough, and he kept changing her with plastic surgery, dental work, and fake tans. She pats two generous stones that jut out like her fake breasts, stuck in their ever perky state. She was a caricature of her former self not understanding why he wanted her this way, until she saw his secretary. She had been sculpted to remind him of that woman . . . his mistress. It was enough to fool him, to recapture tenderness. His genuine smiled returned, instead of the white picket fence at the mouth of Hell. He lavished her with clothes and jewels, until his mistress became pregnant.

She fingers an ornate crystal dead center on the neckline and gasps. It looks like a baby! His baby with that woman. His mistress defied him, fleeing to raise the child instead of aborting it. He blamed her for the loss of his mistress, and their union returned to monster and slave.

Her skin, once glowing liquid bronze, turned sallow like the inside of a used ashtray. All hope drained out of her, like her own baby so many years before.

She twirls, sweeping away the dread. Standing tall, she admires her image, a satisfied smile displayed. Yes, she decides, this dress is perfect for the occasion. She undoes the frock with renewed vigor, letting it fall to rest silently at her feet. The place her husband will be the next time she wears it.

Returning the black dress to its place in her closet, the front door opens and slams shut. Redressing, she hears the shuffling footsteps progress into the house.

"You're home early. Not feeling well?" she calls, already knowing the answer to her question. "Maybe something to eat will help."

"Hope it tastes better than the rest of your dishes lately," her husband says with a snarl.

She catches a glimpse of her reflection sporting an all-knowing smirk. Almost skipping out of the room, she replies, "It's almost done now, honey. It's a new recipe . . . and I hear this one is to die for."

Donna Leiss *has been in love with reading, writing, and music since she was a little girl. They all have played a key role in keeping her sane over the years—at least, as sane a writer can be. She currently resides in Middletown, PA with her husband and two Siberian huskies, where she continues to write short stories, poems, and song lyrics. Feel free to connect with the author on Twitter @dllwrites.*

THE CANDY FACTORY

by Catherine Jordan

You'd think a tour through a candy factory would lead to chocolaty, sugary awesomeness. I did.

I have five cavities. "It's genetic," I heard the dentist tell my mom. That means even though I brush my teeth every night—well, mostly every night to be totally honest—I still get cavities because my dad got them when he was a kid.

My mom and dad told me I wasn't allowed to go to the candy factory. "I absolutely forbid it," my mom said, then gave my dad a hard glare. He returned her glare, and said, "You know we can't forbid him." Then my dad grasped me by the shoulders, looked me in the eyes and said, "We've always told you to be good boy. I hope you are."

I figured they were trying to keep me from going and getting more cavities. But since the dentist pretty much said I'd get them no matter what, I hopped on my bike when I got the text from Sid:

lots of free candy. meet at my house.
bike 2 factory from there.

Sid lived two doors down, right next to Mrs. Adler. He was a year older than me, and his real name was Eddie. Everyone called him Sid because that was the name of the bully in the movie *Toy Story* who tortured kid's toys. Sid tortured animals.

I rode my bike into the shade of Sid's garage, and saw Mrs. Adler's new kitten stray inside. Sid saw it, too. Before

I had a chance to nudge the kitten back out, Sid closed the door.

"Here, kitty, kitty," Sid called with a gentle voice. When it approached, he rubbed his hand down the kitten's white back, then snatched its tail and swung it over his head like a lasso. Sid let the tail go, launching the kitten. It hit the cement wall with a dull thud. "Whoa! A cat that doesn't land on its feet. Look!" The kitten darted with a limp under the shelving in the garage.

Sid lay on his stomach and jabbed a broom handle under the shelving. Blood stained the kitten's white face, and it licked at a crooked paw.

"It's hurt," I said, yanking the broom out of Sid's hand. "Leave it alone."

I threw the broom aside and opened his garage door. "C'mon. Let's go," I said, hoping the kitten would make its escape, which it did.

"Hey!" Sid yelled. "You let it get away!"

I hopped on my bike. "I thought you wanted to go to the factory," I said.

"Yeah, okay," Sid replied. "Let's get out of here. My mom's making barf-loaf for dinner. Think I'll pass, thank you."

We rode at a steady pace until a red brick building came into view. "Beat you to it!" Sid yelled.

Our bike tires skidded to a stop on faded, cracked, pavement. A red brick building loomed just ahead.

"Holy shit," Sid said, staring upward, his mouth agape. "It's huge."

The building stretched so high, I couldn't tell where its rooftop ended.

A dented, bent metal sign that read, **CANDY**, clanged against the façade as it swung in the hot breeze. Each bang was followed by a squawk from a bunch of crows circling a tall black smokestack. A dark puff whooshed from the smokestack, scattering the birds.

"Look at all those broken windows," I said.

"They look like open mouths with jagged teeth," Sid said.

"Yeah," I said, "They kinda do."

The bricks were stained black around the windows, and they sagged on top of each other, as if ready to tumble in the next gust of wind.

I stole a glance over my shoulder. The sun shone bright in the distance behind us, but there were dark clouds hanging over the factory and the sky above it was gray. My arms broke out in goose bumps. "There's no one else here. And the front door is boarded up. Are you sure this is the right place?"

"Yeah, I'm sure," Sid said as he jumped off his bike, letting it fall to the pavement with a clang. "We're supposed to go around the back."

"I'm not sure I want to go in there," I said, gripping my handlebars tight. "This place is creepy."

Sid rolled his eyes. "Don't tell me you're chicken."

"I'm not chicken," I said.

"C'mon, chicken," Sid said, taunting me as he started walking. "Hey, I hear people!" he called as he neared the building's corner. "Meet you in back, if you're not afraid."

I wasn't ready to get off my bike, and expected to see Sid run out from around the corner any second, when I heard an echo of laughter. "Sid!" I called. With a sigh, I peddled closer, and heard more laughter. I crept closer. Music. Circus music.

I leaned my bike against the factory's brick wall, and then ran around the corner. A cluster of bright balloons hit me in the face. "Sorry," said the boy holding balloons. "Here," he said, offering me one as he tried to untangle a ribbon string.

"No thanks," I said, dazed.

Cotton candy and lemonade and popcorn stands dotted the parking lot. The sweet smell of funnel cake had my mouth watering. Vendors handed over balloons to anyone who asked. Kids wandered into a line which lead to a back door. A wooden sign staked in the ground at the door read:

Tour the Candy Factory

There were at least a hundred kids waiting. Sid was already at the front of the line with a big grin. He had obviously cheated the line.

"I heard a guy lost a hand in one of the machines," said the boy in front of me.

"Oh yeah? My friend told me a piece of glass fell into a chocolate bar. Someone ate it and choked to death," said the girl beside me, laughing.

Allison Damon stood behind Sid with her arms crossed, biting her bottom lip. I saw a couple guys checking her out. Her long hair hung down her tight, yellow T-shirt. Her blue eyes were rimmed in the same dark eyeliner she always wore. She sure was pretty, but no one liked her.

She threw spit-wads on the bus, aiming at the kids sitting up front. In class, she slumped in her desk chair. Teachers started the year off by asking her to sit up, but she responded by giving them the finger. Yeah, Allison got sent to the principal's office, a lot. She said she didn't care.

Sid looked toward me, waving me up. I shook my head.

The boy in front of me said, "Go ahead. I'm leaving. The line is taking too long."

"Nah," I said. "I know that girl up there. She'd be mad if I had cut in line."

"You mean Allison Damon? She threw gum in my hair. My mom had to get it cut out, and then gave me a bad haircut. Allison made fun of me for weeks."

Sid waved again. "Get up here," Sid mouthed.

"Definitely jip Allison," said the boy. "I know that kid in front of her, Sid. She won't give him any crap. I'm leaving. Bye."

I moseyed my way through the line toward Sid. "Excuse me. Pardon me. Mind if I move ahead?" A couple kids eyeballed me. "My friend is holding my spot," I said loud for all to hear.

"Hey!" Allison yelled when I cut in front of her. "You're not jipping the line, too."

"Screw you, Allison," Sid said. "I already told you I'm in a hurry cuz I gotta take a leak, so we're next, unless you want us pissing all over your shoes."

Allison's jaw fell open at Sid's threat. A pink wad of gum balanced on her tongue. Her eyes narrowed into slits as she clamped her mouth shut, chewed, and snapped her gum.

"And I better not find any gum in my hair," Sid warned.

"Or what?" Allison asked, snapping loudly.

"I heard you just got a dog," Sid said. "It's a poodle, right? I hear that thing yapping every morning when I ride by your house on my way to school. Sure would be a shame if anything were to happen to it."

Allison's eyes widened. "If anything ever happens to my dog, I swear I will—"

"Next!" called a voice from behind the open door.

Sid slapped me on the back. "That's us," he said.

A hand reached out the door, offering candy bars. We snapped up the bars, ripped open the foil packaging, took a greedy bite, and stepped through the door.

It was dark inside, and my eyes took a few seconds to adjust. The door slammed shut behind us, and I heard it latch. My stomach twisted, and the chocolate turned to chalk in my mouth. "Sid," I whispered, dropping my candy bar to the floor. "It doesn't smell like chocolate in here. It smells like meat. Maybe this wasn't such a good idea."

I don't know if he didn't hear me, or if he was ignoring me, but Sid continued to wolf down his candy bar as he stared at the sign in front of us.

Chocolate Tank. Bungee Jumping.
Must be 18, or have parent's permission.

"Ah, man. This is awesome!" Sid said through a black mouthful of chocolate.

We were standing on a platform. I leaned over and saw a tank below filled with dark liquid. "That's a long drop," I said.

A woman stepped out of the shadows. Dressed in white coveralls, she was maybe in her twenties, tall, with light brown hair wrapped under a hair net. She didn't smile. Her nostrils flared, and she looked down at us like she was a know-it-all superior.

"Well?" the woman asked.

"Well what?" Sid asked, defiant.

"I can tell you're not eighteen," she said. "If you want to Bungee jump into the tank, then you must have your parent's permission."

"My parents know I'm here," Sid snapped. "They told me I could come. I'll go first." Sid ribbed me with his elbow. "Cuz my friend is chicken."

Our guide helped Sid strap on a bungee cord. I'll never forget the look on his face, the excitement in his eyes. "Here I go!" he yelled as he dove off the ledge.

Sid dropped like a torpedo. In the split second before he hit the surface, a crocodile's head popped out, followed by another and another. The croc's long jaws opened to display rows of jagged teeth. Sid screamed as they leapt at him. For a moment he was caught, pulled, then released.

The taut bungee cord yanked him back up toward the platform, and I saw two blood-squirting stumps; one at his wrist, the other at his elbow. Sid looked toward me, terror replacing the excitement in his eyes. His face contorted into a cringe as he dropped again toward the tank and the crocs.

This time the croc's jaws sunk into his shoulders, and they tore off a bloody chunk. He bobbed up and down again—all while screaming—as they wrestled with his torso. Finally there was nothing left but the red cord swinging in the air. Sid was gone! Gone. I leaned over and stared down into the tank. My discarded candy bar fell, twirling like a maple seed, landing on top of a croc's nose.

"An animal abuser?" asked my guide.

I was too shocked to answer, to do anything. I should've gone into hysterics at that point, but my thought process was all messed up.

I heard a clank of machinery and almost lost my balance on the platform as the tank of dark liquid filled with sinking crocs—air bubbles rising from their nostrils—shifted to the left on a rotation.

Sandboxes, swings, merry go rounds and picnic tables swung into view below.

Allison was beckoned through with a candy bar. She had a choice of slides from which to choose her descent to the playground. Allison pointed at a corkscrew slide that boasted a fast and long ride down its shiny metal surface.

"Don't," I said, shaking. "It's not what you think."

"Screw you," Allison said, spitting her gum at me. It bounced off my nose. Allison sat on the ledge and shoved off. Down and around she went, bellowing with laughter at each curve.

Allison came to a sudden halt at the last curve; she was caught in something, but I couldn't tell what it was, at first. Her face contorted as a cut appeared through her open-mouthed smile. The weight of her body and the pitch at which she sat forced her through the invisible entrapment. Then the blood ran. As she continued her decent, her body left behind red streaks and slid apart into pieces. Allison's body landed on the ground, her body collapsing into the sandbox like a slivered heap of raw meat.

"A sarcastic, mean girl whose words cut through others like the wires that cut through her," said the woman.

Allison had become entangled in a trap of razor thin wires. Sid was eaten by crocs. What was in store for me, I wondered as I took a step backward.

"I am in charge of who enters," said the woman who I had thought to be our tour guide. "And who leaves. I decide what the sinner has coming to them."

"What do I deserve?" I asked. My crotch went warm. I looked down to see I had peed in my pants.

"Every execution deserves a witness," she said, solemn faced. "You witnessed their crimes, so you witnessed their punishments." The door opened. "You can leave anytime you want."

Dread left me in degrees, and was replaced with relief.

I bolted out the door and stumbled out of the line, pushing people out of my way. "Don't go in!" I screamed, "You have to get out of here! It's not a candy factory."

"No way," I heard someone reply, "My parents told me this is the last night to take the tour. The factory is closing after tonight."

I ran through a cloud of balloons toward my bike. All the way home, I couldn't get the smell of blood out of my noose.

I burst through the front door, crying. "M-o-o-o-o-m!"

"Where have you been?" my mom asked, expressionless as she awaited my answer. "Was Eddie with you? Mrs. Adler called. Do you know what happened to her cat?"

"Yes," I sobbed. "It was him. But he didn't deserve to be eaten by crocodiles!"

"Crocodiles? Where were you two?"

I didn't know what to say. Where, exactly, had I been? "The candy factory?" I whispered.

"Oh my," she said, enveloping me in her arms. "Your father and I warned you. Come on, let's clean you up." Then more to herself she quietly said, "Well, I suppose Eddie's parents will figure it out when he doesn't come home for supper."

"Figure what out?" I asked, shaking as I followed her toward the bathroom.

My mom sat on the tub's edge, took a deep breath and said, "The factory reopens every twenty years in the early summer, closing when there's no one left in line. It's original to our city, and parents have adhered to its coming and going ever since the summer of 1821. Do you remember from history class what happened back in 1821?"

"Yes," I said. We were learning about factories and the industrial revolution in school. "That's the year the first factory was built in our city. But it burnt down."

"It was a candy factory. That fire spread out of control," my mom said. "And lots of people died. Almost half of the city. The fire was set by children, and not by accident."

I wrinkled my eyebrows and shifted my feet. "Why?"

"Have you ever heard the term, 'bad seed?'" my mom asked, her face pale.

"I think so. I'm not sure."

"A bad seed refers to a child who has not turned out so good," my mom explained as she turned on the bath water. "Kind of like a seed you thought was a flower but wound up becoming a weed. Weeds choke flowers, so you have to pull them up and get rid of them. Those children who set that fire were bad seeds. And now the factory—or maybe it's the victims' ghosts—rids our town of the bad seeds. Warnings don't help; parents know their children will hear its call. I did when I was your age, so did your father. We hope our children will return, like you did, but some parents know not to bother.

"You'll miss Eddie," she said and pulled a towel out of the cabinet. "Some of your other friends, too." She placed the towel on the edge of the tub. The color had returned to her face. She smiled, and said, "You're home; you're a good boy. Come down for supper when you're all clean."

Catherine Jordan *is the author of the horror novels,* Seeking Samiel, *and* The Bookseller's Secret. *She edits and writes in different genres and is a contributor to* TheBurg Magazine, *a variety of anthologies, and on-line publications. Catherine has been a judge for the Bram Stoker Award and the ITW Young Adult Award. She also facilitates writing courses and critique groups. Catherine lives in Pennsylvania with her husband and five children.*

THE LIGHT OF NIGHT

by Mark Boerma

On this particular evening, an astute observer looking at the moon would notice that it's blue and conclude a dust storm is occurring somewhere. However, tonight, not anyone listening to the weather forecast would be aware. No weather satellite is picking up any cloud formation that would obstruct visibility. Depending on the level of inebriation, the color of the moon or a developing dust storm would be of little or no interest to an intoxicated person. If you put a drunken person behind the wheel of a self-driving car, they probably would not have any concern about running somebody over. Such is the case of this slightly buzzed couple, Mick and Loretta. Tonight is Halloween, and there is a blue moon.

"Some place to have a party, out in the middle of nowhere," Loretta sarcastically remarks to Mick.

"You don't mind that we had to leave the party early, do you?" Mick asks.

"No," Loretta says with a yawn. "I told you I have an early appointment tomorrow. Besides, I've had a long day. I'm ready for bed."

"Shit!" Mick stares in the rearview mirror. "Did you see that kid?"

"No." Loretta turns and looks out onto the lonely road.

"I saw some kid, big kid, dressed like an alien. What's he doing out here this late?"

"We're headed out toward Area 51. There's no kids out this way. Your mind is playing tricks on you," Loretta says. "You must be as tired as I am."

"Yeah, thank God for self-driving cars. But wait till you hear the conversation I overheard between Frank and Mort tonight."

"Frank is a chemist, right?" Loretta asks.

"Right," Mick says. "And Mort invests in companies that develop and improve the technology for self-driving cars, like the one I'm driving."

"But you're not really driving it; the car's driving. All right, go ahead."

"Frank," Mick continues, "who by the way was dressed as some frozen Butter Ball turkey, was telling Mort, who was dressed as 1940's style mystery man, that he invented a resin capable of creating a plastic bag that has a peculiar function."

Loretta then says, "Oh wait, I think I saw Mort. His costume was a 1940's style newspaper reporter. I noticed a card in his hat with the word 'Scoop' on it. And he carried that newspaper under his arm the entire evening."

"Oh yeah? Okay. Anyway, this particular function, which occurs when you place an object in the bag and the bag experiences an impact, disintegrates everything inside the bag, including the bag."

Loretta, rolling her eyes, says, "That's nonsense. Resins are nonvolatile. I think you've had too much to drink."

Mick's face reddens. "I'm just relaying a message."

"Personally," Loretta says, "I think it is part of an elaborate scheme so that you men don't have to take out the trash."

"Loretta, are you listening?"

"Yes, I'm listening."

"Frank mentioned that there are some bugs to be worked out. During laboratory testing when the bag disintegrates upon impact, some undesirable byproducts occur. There is a bright flash of light and a pile of dust remains. Top secret stuff. I'm not supposed to be telling anyone, so—"

"Watch out!" Loretta screams. "You're gonna hit that trick-or-treater!"

"Mort?" Mick yells, confused by what he is seeing.

At that moment, even though the impact was so bright it blinded them, Mick knew he ran over someone. He and Loretta are dazed and momentarily frozen in their seats.

"I hit Mort." Mick says.

"What would Mort be doing out here?" asks Loretta, with horror on her face.

Mick and Loretta jump out of the car and run toward the body on the ground.

"Hey, are you all right?" Mick asks. "It's so dark. I can't tell if he's hurt, or dazed, or . . ."

"I can't see a thing," says Loretta.

Mick runs back to the car and digs his flashlight out of the glove compartment. He shines the light on his car. There are no damages. He lets out a sigh of relief, thinking whomever he hit must surely be okay.

"Mick," says Loretta, "Come over here."

Mick's light then lands first on Loretta, who is kneeling by a pile of dust. A slight breeze comes along and scatters it.

"That's odd," says Mick. "What did I hit?"

"I don't know," says Loretta.

He and Loretta decide to go for a brief stroll around the area. Mick notices a folded newspaper on the ground. He picks it up and sees two articles on the bottom half of the front page, one regarding a mysterious death of an investment banker and another about suspicious trading activity at Google Cars. Mick flips the newspaper over to the top half to see the following headline: "Flashes of Light Seen Near Area 51 on Halloween Night."

Mark Boerma *is a programmer analyst at Keystone Insurers Group, Northumberland, PA. He received his B.S. degree from King's College, Wilkes-Barre, PA before eventually becoming a self-employed consultant in 1991. After his term as a consultant, he accepted a position with Godiva Chocolatier. He currently resides in Hazle Township, PA. He can be contacted at mboerma@ptd.net.*

A LOGICAL MAN

by Sandy Nork

I am a logical man. Truly, I am.

I am a realist. I only believe in what I can touch.

But . . .

But.

My mother, my beautiful mother, passed away five years ago. I miss her terribly every day. I see her clearly in my mind, tall, slender, her dark brown hair framing her face. But I know she's dead and nothing will change that.

I also know that she woke me from a deep sleep a few nights ago. My bed shifted and creaked. My mother was sitting on the corner of my bed. But I know that a ghost, if she were a ghost, wouldn't have the weight to cause my bed to shift and creak. Still, I woke right up, eyes wide, my breathing harsh in my own ears. And there she sat, in a skirt and button-up blouse with the sleeves rolled above her elbows, the way she always wore them.

"Honey, it's all right," she said. "Everything is all right. I am fine. You are fine. And your father . . . I'll take care of him, too. We'll all be happy. Now go back to sleep."

I know she loved me. I know she still does.

I'm not quite sure how, but I did manage to fall back to sleep. Maybe because she calmed me, so I guess I just drifted off.

In the morning, I went to work at the firm, losing myself in the numbers, the numbers that are so soothing, so organized.

I always want to be organized. My mother taught me that. Even when I was a child, she wanted me to not cause havoc or leave a scattered mess behind me. I did that sometimes, left things a mess. But my father was much worse. To him she used to say, "It would be easier to burn this house down than to clean up after you."

I went about my business at work, never telling anyone what happened, not even my father. Especially not my father.

Where my mother was beautiful and caring and encouraging to me, my father was hard and angry and punishing. I could never please him, not ever. Not as a child and certainly not as an adult.

I don't see much of my father. We keep different hours. He's a laborer who gets up at 5:30 in the morning to catch whatever ride he can to the job site. My mother told me that when I was a baby, he managed a work crew for a construction company, but the company went out of business. It was hard on him and he changed, she said. It seemed to me that it must have been my fault somehow. He was and is angry. Always.

He works his eight or ten or twelve hours, then goes to the bar with his fellow workers and drinks away whatever money he earned that day. He comes home late, having eaten little or nothing, and roots through the refrigerator. He usually eats whatever he can scrounge with the refrigerator door hanging open. Doesn't bother with a plate. Doesn't bother with utensils, either, unless dinner is soup.

That night, he didn't come home until after I went to bed. He was gone before I got up. Maybe he never came home, I don't know. I just know I didn't run into him until a few days later. He was eating leftover brisket with his fingers, juices running down his face.

I tried to talk to him.

Pointless.

"You weak, pathetic excuse for a son," he said to me. "You're so lazy you can't even find a real job. Son, huh. You sit at a desk all day with the other girls probably helping them polish their nails! Do you answer the phone, too? Get the real bosses' coffee? You wouldn't know how to handle a shovel if I hit you over the head with one." He ate another bite of brisket and said, with his mouth full, "I oughta do that. Knock some sense into you."

He pushed by me on his way toward the couch in the living room where he obviously intended to finish his meal. An open bottle of beer and a partial bottle of whiskey were already sitting on the coffee table, waiting for him.

I closed the refrigerator door.

"You're not my son. If your mother was here, she'd tell you. You're some other guy's seed, that's for sure. They were too smart to hang around to see what kind of lame bastard you are."

My mother would not have said that.

"She would have told me long ago if that was true," I said. No, I was sure I belonged to the man with juices dripping down his hands and onto the floor. "You're my father, much as I hate the thought."

"You asshole!" he said, then returned to where I stood and pushed me into the door jamb. I glimpsed a vision of my mother standing behind the door. She nodded to me.

The next thing I knew, my fingers were around his throat. I was surprised at how their length seemed to wrap just right around his entire neck. I pushed down with my thumbs into his windpipe and felt how easy it was to close off his air.

But he was a fighter and, with veins popping on his forehead and around his bulging eyes, he fought to knock my arms away. I let my thumbs up just enough for him to get some air and sputter, "Bastard!" into my face. Horrified at what I realized I was doing, I pushed him away, and I backed into the kitchen. He stumbled into the living room. He must have lost his footing because I heard him hit the coffee table, knocking the bottles to the floor with a crash.

Silence.

I waited for a few seconds, and when there was no sound of rage following the crash, I peeked around the door. My father was sprawled across one side of the coffee table and half onto the floor. I thought he was dead, but then I heard throaty snores coming from deep in his chest. He just passed out. My fault. I had choked him almost to the point of death, but he must have hit the corner of the coffee table because his head was bleeding.

I sighed angrily. Not only did I have to clean up his mess on the floor, I would also have to bandage his head.

I set to work on the floor first, to get the blood and alcohol sponged up and the food swept out of the way, but his head would not stop bleeding. By the time I managed to find bandages, he had slipped into a deeper sleep and his snoring had stopped. A coma, I thought. I shifted him off the coffee table and onto the couch and blotted up the residue from under his body. I was surprised that the whiskey bottle didn't break and luckily the cap kept it from spilling, unlike the beer.

I went upstairs to my room, overwhelmed with what to do next. Too many courses of action, too many what-ifs. I was exhausted. I lay down to think, only for a minute I told myself, but of course I fell asleep. A gentle hand on my shoulder woke me.

"You should get up now. There's more to do."

It was dark. Hours must have passed. My head was thick with sleep. The voice was familiar. I blinked and when I finally got a look at the speaker, I didn't know what to think.

"Don't look so surprised," my mother said, and helped me to stand. "You have to clean up the rest of this mess. You know what to do."

Did I?

Yes, I did. Mother did not like messes.

I went downstairs with Mother whispering to me, "Get the whiskey bottle."

In the kitchen I found the whiskey where I'd left it. I took it into the living room and put it where my father would want it, on the coffee table.

"No," she said, leaning into my face, wrapping one arm around my shoulders. "That's not where you should put it. Let me show you."

Mother disappeared into the kitchen and returned with a box of wooden matches. She opened the whiskey and poured it all over the couch. Then she lit the matches and, one by one, dropped them around my father.

I watched for a few minutes as flames boiled up from the surface of the couch. I was tired again. So, so tired.

***

Chief Adams crouched in front of the young man wrapped in a blanket who was sitting on the ground. Adams patted him on the shoulder, then stood and waved the medical technicians toward him as they filed out of the ambulance.

"I think he's pretty disoriented," Adams told them.

The medics bent over the man. "From the look of his clothes he must have been pretty close to the fire," one of them said.

"Yup," Adams said.

Adams studied the smoking house. One of his men ran toward him at an ungainly trot, the weight of his equipment slowing him down.

"There's a body in there, Chief," said the firefighter. "First floor."

"I was afraid of that," Adams said. "Tell the sheriff to call the coroner."

The firefighter nodded and ran back toward the rubble of the house. Neighbors clustered to gossip and gawk, their voices a low, urgent din.

"And get those people to move back!" Adams called out.

The sound of a chilling laugh among the rubberneckers caught his ear. When Adams looked to see who it might be, he could have sworn he saw a tall, thin woman with dark brown hair in a skirt and button-front shirt with the sleeves rolled up to her elbows.

Sandy Nork *is a writer, researcher, and editor from New Cumberland, PA. She also does grant consulting and writing for nonprofit agencies. She has published nonfiction in newspapers and journals. Her husband, Bill, is a musician who inspired her current fiction work-in-progress, a suspense novel about a valuable guitar. Sandy calls herself a musical tourist, coffee drinker, yoga enthusiast, baking* *devotee, technology aficionado, trained librarian, and friend of all dogs. Well, most dogs. You can find her on Twitter as @novelgal and on Facebook as Sandy Nork.*

BREAKFAST, INTERRUPTED

A script by Ann Elia Stewart

A harried, young mom and caregiver brings her confused grandpa and young son to a large, urban toy store only to lose them in the holiday bustle. She follows clues left by their discarded breakfast, but as the crowds swell, she grows more frantic as each clue seems to lead her in circles.

FADE IN

EXT. TIMES SQUARE SIDEWALK - DAY

Shot opens on a close-up of A MCDONALD'S BAG in the veiny, gnarled hand of an elderly man, a gray, flannel robe sleeve cuffs half his hand. Shot travels to another MCDONALD'S BAG, this time clutched by two hands belonging to a small child, his bright blue robe sleeve nearly swallowing both hands. We now see the elderly man, GRANDPA, and the small blond, blue-eyed child, FINN, 3, walk side-by-side behind JUNIE, young mom, late 20s. She's fresh-faced, pretty but simply dressed and parts the bustle of the crowds for her grandfather and young son, who wear robes over their sweater and jeans, superheroes in spirit.

Junie stops at the entrance of Toys 'R Us and the two behind her come to an abrupt halt as if following her in a trance.

She turns around to address them.

JUNIE. If we get separated for any reason, come right back to the front of the store. (*She points to the doors.*) Right here.

They nod.

JUNIE (cont'd). Okay, troops, let's go shop!
INT.- ENTRANCE/TOYS 'R US - DAY
A FERRIS WHEEL inside the store, already in motion, catches Finn's attention. He drifts toward it, still clutching his McDonald's bag. Grandpa's attention veers to the spectacle of Christmas all around him. Junie runs after Finn, grabs his hand, brings him back to Grandpa. Junie approaches everything as if she has only an hour to live.
JUNIE. Grandpa? Listen carefully. This is the only time I have to shop, so please remember to look after Finn, too. I don't want to have to spend the morning hunting for him.
GRANDPA, *holding his bag up.* Where's the restaurant in here? I wanna sit to eat these pancakes.
JUNIE. This a *toy store*, Grandpa. Just try to eat as we shop.
The front door opens continuously, spitting shoppers into the lobby.
JUNIE (cont'd) (*fretful*). C'mon guys, times a'wastin'!
Junie leads, with Finn and Grandpa hopping on the escalator behind her, depositing them to a floor filled with action figure displays. A lifelike, full-sized T-Rex can be seen in the background, as if he's scanning for his next victim. Finn tugs Grandpa's sleeve.
FINN (*enthusiastically pointing*). Dino-shore!
He starts drifting over to the T-Rex, but Junie scoops him up before he gets too far.
GRANDPA. Aw, let him see the thing.
Junie scans the growing crowd around the dinosaur. She bends down to Finn.
JUNIE. Finn, you *must* hold Grandpa's hand all the time.
Finn holds his bag up for her to take. Junie takes it, fishes out a hash brown patty, hands it to him. She hands Finn's bag to Grandpa, who carries it along with his own.
Grandpa takes Finn's other hand and starts to walk toward the T-Rex.
JUNIE. Wait, Grandpa! We'll meet at the entrance—do you remember where that is?
Grandpa gives her a give-me-a-break look.

JUNIE (cont'd). Let's meet in twenty minutes, then, that's 9:30. Once we're all together, we can shop some more.

She tugs Grandpa's robe collar.

JUNIE (cont'd). You got that?

Grandpa breaks away, being tugged by Finn. He looks back at Junie, barely gets out—

GRANDPA. Got it!

INT.- ENTRANCE/TOYS 'R US - DAY

Insert: Cell phone face: 9:30

Junie paces. From her POV: we scan the FERRIS WHEEL and see many children and adults riding the cars, but no Finn or Grandpa.

Junie walks to the bottom of the escalator, again from her POV:, people pour onto it, but no Finn or Grandpa.

From behind Junie

CHILD. Mommy!

Junie whips around. An Asian child runs toward his mother. Junie's split-second relief dissipates. She pulls out her phone.

INSERT: 9:40

Shoppers continue to come and go, Christmas music loops ad nauseum. She finds a bench beside a shady-looking man with long, stringy hair, greasy overcoat, baggy sweats, sandals worn over grimy socks. He's fishing around inside a McDonald's bag, same size as Finn's and Grandpa's.

Junie bursts from the bench in the direction of the escalators, heads upstairs.

INT - DINOSAUR AREA

Junie thrashes her way through a crowd, now five deep. She catches sight of something we cannot yet see.

SHOPPER. Hey, hey! What the hell? Enough with the pushing!

Junie ignores the shopper, keeps trying to penetrate the crowd, eventually makes her way to the front row, the thumping, undulating T-Rex underscoring her efforts. A MIDDLE-AGED WOMAN blocks her advance.

WOMAN (*nasty*). This is MY spot, get out of here!

JUNIE (*taken aback*). I-I'm looking for my family.

WOMAN (cont'd). Yeah, right, good one.

The woman shoves her, but Junie moves sideways, finding a gap; she slips into it.

We now see what she has been focusing on:

INSERT: A BLUE BELT FROM A CHILD'S ROBE hanging on the rail of the dock leading up to the T-Rex.

She steps ahead, but a SECURITY GUARD rushes her.

SECURITY GUARD. Lady, you can't go in there!

Junie manages to snatch the belt from the railing.

JUNIE (cont'd). I can't find my family! (*She shouts over the din.*) They were supposed to meet me and they didn't and now—

SECURITY GUARD. Whoa! Slow down, lady!

He activates his walkie-talkie.

Junie catches a scent of food. She literally follows her nose and scurries away from the guard.

SECURITY GUARD. Hey, lady. . .

Junie continues to follow her nose and runs headlong into a POPCORN MACHINE, popcorn bursting from its core into a transparent cage. From a movie playing behind her, we hear Yoda's famous line:

YODA. Do or do not. There is no try.

She drops against the machine.

JUNIE (*quiet, scared*). Finn. Grandpa.

The security guard winds his way through the crowd of dino gawkers. Junie recovers, eludes him, continues toward LegoLand, but slips on something. She bends down, picks it up. It looks like a CRUNCHED CONTAINER OF BUTTER, the kind from a take-out breakfast. She's bolstered, moves ahead into

INT. - LEGOLAND

where she's surrounded with giant displays of the Chrysler Building, Empire State Building, King Kong—

JUNIE (*shouting now*). Finn! Grandpa!

She heads toward the Arc de Triomphe Lego creation, entering into a Parisian display where accordion music plays, no crowds. She spots a small container of something by the "Eiffel Tower," picks it up.

INSERT: A McDonald's maple syrup packet.

She throws it into one of her shopping bags, rushes forward into a Little Tykes area. She stops cold. From Junie's POV:

the robed backs of Finn and Grandpa, sitting at a Little Tykes table in Little Tykes chairs, enjoying what remains of their PANCAKE breakfast. Finn's missing his belt. Grandpa turns around as he hears someone approach, greets Junie with warm surprise.

GRANDPA. We found the restaurant!

FADE TO BLACK

Ann Elia Stewart *received a fellowship in fiction from the Pennsylvania Council of the Arts and teaches creative writing. She developed a curriculum for and teaches creative writing at the Capital Area School for the Arts Charter School in Harrisburg, PA. Ann's novel,* Twice a Child, *explores Alzheimer's and Parkinson's diseases.*

SCENT AND SCENTABILITY

by Angela Binner

Brown sugary sweetness, buttery undertones, fresh hot popcorn, and just a hint of salt . . . Mmm. Claire's caramel corn. I could almost taste it as I walked toward her stand at Mean Mike's Flea Market that Friday afternoon, back when I still lived at home.

"Sweet mother of pearl." I stopped and a woman plowed right into me from behind.

"Sorry," I said, as she muttered something about my needing to watch where I was going.

But that was the problem. I had watched where I was going and where I went should have been Claire's. I looked around.

"Where's Claire? Who are you?" I asked the gray-haired woman who stood behind a battered old table filled with bottles.

She shrugged and said, "Don't know any Claire, but I got a special on perfumes." She smiled as if proud to show off the gap where her front tooth should have been. "Half off all of 'em." She pointed out several bottles. "I got Giorgio, real popular, Charlie, Lauren, and old standards like White Shoulders. What are you looking for?"

I was looking for caramel corn, but since I was there, I studied the bottles. "Half off, huh?" I reached for one. "Wait." I shook my head. "These are half empty."

"And I told you half off, and today, any one for ten bucks."

"Oh. Uh huh. I see." Well, no sale from me.

I turned to walk away when one bottle caught my eye. I'd never seen a perfume like it before. Blood red colored, it had a strange ear-shaped green lid. I picked it up, twisted off the top, and took a whiff. Very familiar.

"This is Sweet Honesty from Avon. I already have a bottle of it at home."

"Avon?" The woman snatched it from my hand. "Something's wrong with your nose. Perfumes like I sell go for a fortune at Neiman Marcus and Lord & Taylor. This particular perfume," she held the bottle beside her face and patted it, "can cost a lot more."

Neiman Marcus and Lord & Taylor? How would an old woman who sold half-used bottles of perfumes at a flea market know about those stores? I only knew of their existence because Zaber's, the factory where I worked, shipped to them.

"Somebody's knocking, should I let him in. Lord it's the devil, would you look at him . . .[1]" From the radio at another stand.

That song reminded me of the blue-eyed, blue-jeaned devil I wished would come knockin' at my door: Darce Clancy. I sighed and remembered his promise to call sometime in March after our third date. Never heard a word. Then Jimmy Batz told me at work that Darce was pretty hot with Ellen, the youngest Zaber girl. I'd tried to get more information, but other than telling me they were dating, Jimmy wouldn't say much.

"Hey, you gonna stand there dreamy eyed? Then go somewhere else cause I got other customers."

"Oh yeah?" I glanced over my shoulder. People walked by without looking toward her stand. "Where?"

She tilted her head back, looked at me through narrowed eyes, and with a little green make-up, standing like that, she might have passed for the Wicked Witch of the West.

I looked down at the blood red bottle, and that's when I saw the price.

1Gillespie, J. /Penney, E. /Mattson, E. (1981) Somebody's Knockin' (Recorded by Terri Gibbs). On *Somebody's Knockin'* (vinyl). Universal City, CA: MCA Records.

"Wait a minute. Fifteen dollars? You said half off; half off fifteen is not ten. It's seven fifty. And that one," I pointed to the red bottle, "is less than half full. You want ten dollars for something somebody's already tried, returned, and looks a few steps below worthless?"

I turned to leave but stopped when I felt her hand on my arm.

"I'll be honest," the woman lowered her voice. "That one is different. It's magical, and I don't normally point it out, but you look like you could use some magic." She gave the lid a rub. "I used this one myself. It's how I got this space today."

"Then why not keep it?"

She shrugged. "It runs back to me after it's done its work."

I snorted. Magical perfumes that ran away? Next she'd tell me something really crazy, like Darce would magically reappear in my life.

She continued, her voice back to normal volume, "Well, you gonna buy it or stand there all day? I got other customers."

"So you said." On my left and right, no one near us, but, curious, I leaned toward her. "How can a bottle of perfume have magic?"

The woman smiled and again patted the lid as if it was a favorite pet. "You can see it's different. It's not like the other perfumes."

That much was true. It didn't fit in. It wasn't glitzy especially with that green ear-shaped lid.

"This perfume fills the air with a scent that leads you to know the truth." She leaned closer. "Say you're with a man who loves you. Maybe the perfume will fill the air with the smell of fresh roses. If he hates you, fire."

I picked up the bottle again, and dabbed some on my wrist. It still reminded me of Sweet Honesty.

"I don't know."

I tried to calculate how long I'd have to work to earn ten dollars, but stopped. That was Jimmy's way of thinking.

No Jimmy thoughts, I told myself, not after thinking about Darce. Jimmy with his tall, skinny body, pointy nose, and mud brown eyes, who saw eye-to-eye with my parents on everything was not worth my thoughts. We went out a lot as friends, and then a few days ago a couple gals at work called me naïve to think he didn't like me more than that. Well, I'd have to nip that in the bud.

I looked down at the red bottle and sighed. Ten bucks seemed like a lot, but it was Friday, I'd come to buy caramel corn, and if I couldn't get that, well, it was a unique bottle.

"I'll give you five dollars," I said.

The woman licked her lips. "Eight." She hunched into her shoulders and cackled.

I shot back with, "Six."

"Seven fifty."

"Seven."

"Sold." She cackled again, and I expected to hear, "My pretty."

Instead she reached for the ten I'd fished out of my pocket and took it so fast, I'd have sworn she had the magic to make things disappear. Then her hands reached under the table, and she brought out a wad of bills. She peeled off three and handed them to me, careful two didn't stick together. After a few last pats, she rolled the bottle of magical perfume in newspaper, placed it in a paper bag, and held it out toward me.

"Now be careful," she said as I took the bag. "You might think you want to learn the truth, but maybe you don't."

"Yeah, right. I'll be careful. Hey, since I have some on, what do I smell like?"

She shrugged, smiled, showed that gap again and said, "You smell like promising beginnings."

I snorted too loud and turned away hoping nobody other than the old woman heard, but no one so much as glanced toward us.

Not ready to go home, I looked around at the other stands. My dad would be counting on caramel corn, so I needed a substitute. As I let my eyes roam, I saw someone familiar. Someone who made me hope my hair wasn't frizzy and my mascara hadn't run. No way. It couldn't be, but it was: Darce.

Six-foot four, blue eyes, curly brown hair in tight-fitting blue jeans and white tee-shirt, he stood in front of the pretzel stand, holding a soft pretzel. The old lady said I smelled like promising beginnings, well, Darce was a very promising one.

Deciding my dad would love pretzels, I walked over just as Darce shoved a piece in his mouth.

"Hey, Fran Shaffer," he said with the pretzel inflating his right cheek. "Haven't seen you for awhile."

Even though he looked a little like a six-foot chipmunk with his fat cheek, I still forgot how to get oxygen or speak in his presence.

"Been thinking about you," he said and then swallowed. "A lot." He smiled and topped it with a wink, which helped me ignore the specks of pretzel on his teeth.

"Yeah?" I tamped down a squeal of delight. I was ready to flirt but stopped and cleared my throat. "Wait a minute." I paused. "Thought about you too cause I heard a couple things."

"Like?"

"Like you're dating Ellen Zaber. Maybe that's why you never called when you said you would after we had three dates." I held up three fingers. He looked at them, back at the pretzel, and then into my eyes with his sky blue ones. He smiled and shook his head.

"Nah, Ellen and I, she, we're done. Truth is, Fran, I felt bad about not calling you." He shrugged. "Ellen just needed me."

I didn't want to know for what.

He played with the pretzel in his hands.

"Sort of funny running into you cause I've been wondering." He paused and tapped the pretzel against his knuckles. "You wouldn't care to go out with me again, would you? Give me another chance?"

Had I heard him right?

"You want to go out with me again? Me?" Wait. Why not me? I stood up straight. "I don't know. I'm sort of seeing someone." He needed to do a little more work to get me on a date.

He shoved more pretzel in his mouth. "Oh, yeah, Jimmy. Ellen told me."

"I'm not dating Jimmy," I said almost spitting on him as I did. "I don't know where she came up with that."

Visions of Darce and Ellen in his truck, laughing about how Jimmy and I were well-suited for each other caused my hands to tighten around the bottle of perfume.

"You know, Darce, yeah, I mean, sure. I'll go out. That'd be great."

He smiled, nodded, and shoved yet another piece of pretzel in his mouth.

"Carnival starts tomorrow. You want to go? Think Kitty Wells going to be there." Then he leaned toward me. "Be nice to be with you, Fran."

Me? Carnival? With Darce? Firemen's carnivals were the highlight of summers in Canaan Grove. Walking around the grounds with Darce where everyone could see us? Oh yes.

Then he put his head beside my left ear and said, "You smell good, like ripening summer peaches."

And right then, before I melted away with happiness, before I replied that he smelled like pretzel or something stupid, I said yes. Didn't play hard to get or act unsure. No, I about shouted it, heard him mention being at my house around seven, and never gave a thought that at home on my pocket calendar for tomorrow, I'd written "Jimmy—carnival."

***

A little more than 24 hours later, my blue-eyed, blue-jeaned devil Darce Clancy stood on our front steps. Just seeing him there made the full hour I'd taken to do my hair, half hour for makeup, and money I'd spent on new clothes all worth it. He even made me glad I'd sprung seven bucks for the magical, pre-owned perfume that I'd splashed on.

My dad had answered the door, gave Darce the once over, and almost ran into me when he turned around.

"Thought you were going out with Jimmy tonight," he said. "What's Darce doing here?"

I kept my voice low, hoping Darce couldn't hear. "Jimmy and I are just friends; besides, he called and cancelled."

"When?"

At 22, I didn't need to explain my life to my father. Besides he found out anyway, but since he stood between me and Darce . . .

"This morning. He called this morning."

"Huh." My father rubbed his chin.

My parents loved Jimmy, said he was an honest man and I should hang onto him, meaning he was as good as I was going to get.

"I'll be back later." I stepped out the door so my dad couldn't say another thing. "I'm ready."

Darce gave me a look up and down before he smiled and said, "You look nice, Fran." He stopped and sniffed the air. "You smell that? Funnel cakes. Those things are good."

Of course I smelled funnel cakes. The perfume was working. Darce loved funnel cakes, and he must love me. I was learning the truth. This was going to be a magical night.

"Yeah," I said.

He nodded his head toward the green and white Ford pick-up parked out front. "Well, you ready, my dear?"

The door shut behind me. His "dear" was ready.

Darce led me to the truck, opened the door, and I scooted up and into the cab. It hadn't changed a bit since the last time I'd been in it. No reminders of Ellen, but what did I expect? Her picture? I would have checked the glove compartment just to be sure, but Darce climbed into the driver's seat before I had a chance.

"It's great to be going to carnival," I said after we'd started. "Thought about it all night. You?"

He reached to turn down the radio that came on when he'd started his truck.

"Ought to be good. Kitty Wells draws a crowd," I said, filling in the silence.

"Uh huh. Guess we could have walked. We're almost there already." Darce yawned but didn't cover his mouth. He looked straight out the front of the truck, both hands on the wheel.

Walk and miss a chance to be seen in Darce's truck? Was he crazy? No way.

I waited about 20 seconds for him to add to the conversation, when he didn't, I said, "Been a couple months since we talked. How have you been? Anything new?"

"Nah, you know, family's okay and so's everything else."

I waited for him to continue, maybe ask about my life. Jimmy always did. But Jimmy and I were friends. Of course he'd ask me a lot of questions.

More silence. He obviously had to concentrate on the road, although it was a short trip.

"Lots of people here tonight," he said as we neared carnival.

He was right; the lot was packed. Families, couples, and single people got out of their vehicles and headed onto the carnival grounds. Most carried lawn chairs so they could sit in front of the stage and listen to the music.

Darce inched into the lot and parked away from the grounds and other vehicles, on the grass near a grove of trees that bordered carnival property.

I imagined us sitting in his truck, in the dark after carnival when the lot was empty. He'd lean over, kiss me, kiss me again and again. I'd kiss him back and move closer. He'd then say . . .

"You coming?" He stood outside and held the pickup door opened for me.

When had he done that?

"Yeah. Sure. I'm coming." I swung my legs out and jumped to the ground beside him.

He grabbed my right arm and pulled me close. Was he going to kiss me? I looked up, but all he did was shut the truck's door.

"What's that? Perfume?" He sniffed the air. "You smell like." He stopped and sniffed again. "Roses, yeah, sort of like roses."

Roses? Wasn't that what the witchy woman said love smelled like?

Then he grabbed my hand and smiled. "Well, here we are. Let's go, sweetie."

Had he called me sweetie? Yes, yes, the air did smell of roses, but, wait, no, sort of like roses. More like roses that had wilted and started to rot. That couldn't be. Tonight was magical. We'd be telling our grandkids about our carnival date someday. Must be other smells interfering with the perfume.

We walked to the gate where he let go of my hand to pay but grabbed it again afterward.

He led me to the right toward game booths with crowds surrounding them. Beyond, people lined up outside the fire hall to enter for a hot supper. Further, another line of people waited at a big booth, which had burgers and fries.

On the left, booths of cotton candy, funnel cakes, caramel apples all had crowds around them. For a moment, it reminded me of Mean Mike's, but I shook the thought off and looked at the stage in front of us. It lit the grounds filled with an ocean of lawn chairs brought by Kitty Wells' fans who sat and waited for the show to begin. Taped country music poured out of the loudspeakers and added to the sounds of the night.

The excitement of it—being at carnival with the best looking guy in Canaan Grove, feeling pretty, all hit me at once. Everything took on a strange, magical brightness. I felt like a movie star stepping out of a limo into camera lights. My world could not get any better.

I was about to suggest something to eat, when . . .

"Darce?" That voice, the sound of the sirens that drew sailors to their deaths—Ellen Zaber.

I turned around.

Every strand of blonde hair in place. Jeans emphasized her curvy hips. Three too many buttons undone on her blouse, and her slender arm extended so she could clasp hands with her date, and her date . . . her date . . . Oh no.

It.

Couldn't.

Be.

Jimmy—my Jimmy—but not my friend Jimmy held her hand. The pointy nose was gone, and his eyes were smooth chocolate brown. He stood tall, solid, and handsome with Ellen's hand in his own. He looked . . . desirable.

Something hit me in the heart and more so when Darce dropped my hand and stepped away. Jimmy, however, held Ellen's like if he let go, she'd float into the sky.

Ellen turned toward me. "And, Fran, how are you?"

I opened my mouth to say something then closed it again.

Never would I have expected to see Ellen at carnival with Jimmy holding hands. She was why he'd cancelled our date, the girl who'd stolen Darce from me? And what right did he have for looking so darned good with his eyes glued to her?

Those traitorous eyes glanced toward me. He gave a quick nod, a "hi," and then looked out toward the crowd.

"Jimmy," I said and turned away but looked back and felt another stab in my heart. "Hi, Ellen." I tried to smile but the corners of my mouth wouldn't lift up.

"Didn't know you were coming here, Darce," she said.

Darce kept his eyes on Ellen. His mouth agape, it could have been used as a target for one of the carnival's games.

"Yeah, I, uh." He took a small step back and leaned away from me.

All four of us stood in a line, Jimmy, Ellen, me, and Darce, like targets for a firing squad. I wished the perfume let me know what people thought; I'd have loved to know the thoughts of the other three, one traitor in particular.

"Hey." Jimmy pointed to a booth near us. "Basketball. Should I win you a stuffed animal, El?"

"El" smiled and gave a cheerleader's bounce.

"Oh fun. I'd love that, Jim."

Love? Jim?

Ellen turned to my date. "You guys coming? Darce, you going to win one for Fran?"

Darce looked at me, no smile. "Huh? Yeah? Sure. You want one?"

I didn't say anything for a moment. "Oh, I'd treasure it forever," I said, my voice flat.

I took up the rear behind Darce as the four of us walked to the booth. Jim and El held hands and leaned together, their shoulders touched. El said something and Jim threw his head back to laugh. Sickening.

As we walked up to it, I studied the game. It looked easy enough. Players got a small basketball and had to make five baskets in a row to win a game and a plastic animal. After three wins and three plastic animals, they could trade them for something better, such as a purple stuffed teddy bear or yellow plush pig.

Jimmy tore his hand away from Ellen's. "Here goes." He smiled at her and gave a wink. "Wish me luck."

"Get one for me, Jim. That pink one on the top shelf." She pointed toward a pink teddy bear that beamed down at her, ready to jump into her manicured fingers.

Jimmy paid, took aim, and fired away.

I'd never seen him shoot a basketball. Jimmy wasn't the sports type, but he concentrated, shot, and made each basket. Before long, and in front of several clapping female admirers, he placed the teddy bear into Ellen's hands. She laughed and looked about to lean in for a kiss.

"Lemme try." Darce pushed his way between them.

Darce must have never seen a basketball before let alone shoot one. His efforts sent Ellen into a fit of giggles. Every basket he threw not only didn't go near the net, his final try hit the guy manning the booth's forehead.

"Game's rigged," he said and focused a frown at me as if it was my fault he had a lousy aim and no talent.

"Isn't he the cutest?" Ellen pushed the smiling bear toward Jimmy.

Was she talking about the bear or him?

"Well, since we're all here, why don't we hang out?" She picked up Jimmy's hand. "Fran, Darce, did you guys eat? I was checking out what they had. Why don't we get a burger and fries instead of standing in line for a big dinner at the fire hall?"

Having enough of the evening already, I started to say no, but she cut in.

"I'm buying."

That was the final straw. Darn Ellen Zaber, showing us little people that she could afford to take the hired help out. And how dare she make Jimmy happier than I'd ever seen him with me? And how could he be so happy, smiling at her like that, like she mattered? Did she?

"No, you're not, El," Jimmy said. "I'm buying cause I'm the one celebrating my new job."

"What?" Now my mouth opened and didn't close.

"Yeah." He looked at me. "Going to work for a truck parts company, finally put my mechanical skills to use."

"And that's not all you're celebrating." Ellen's eyes never left Jimmy's face.

He looked down at his feet. "That's not for sure, El."

"Go on. Tell them. It's great news." If she smiled any wider, her face would have cracked in half.

"I put in a bid on a house."

A sharp odor flew up my nose and hit me right at the top of my nasal passage, between my eyes, the smell of sulfur, a match newly lit. I tried to cough it out, but it was stuck. I gagged and blew out my nose, but it wasn't budging, just got worse. I leaned over and hacked like a cat with a fur ball.

"Fran?" Jimmy said as he moved to my side.

"I can't breathe." I held my chest. It was true; my whole body worked at getting rid of the stuck odor and wasn't concerned with getting oxygen. "I don't feel good." The smell seeped into my throat and stomach. "I, I think I'm going to be sick."

Jimmy grabbed my arm as sweat rolled down my forehead and fell onto the grass.

"Take it easy, Fran. Just breathe." He put his hand on my back and rubbed in big circles.

"Let's take her somewhere to sit down," Ellen said. "Darce, go get her something to drink."

"Why? Since when are you Florence Nightingale?"

"Since about the time you didn't care about your date. Now go get her a drink."

The smell grew stronger. My knees went weak. I headed toward the ground, face first.

"I think I'm going to faint." I wanted to cry. I opened my mouth and coughed but nothing moved that smell.

"Fran, listen." Jimmy wrapped his arms around me. "We're going to walk over to the pavilion and sit down."

"No." I shook my head. "I want to go home."

"I'm not letting you go home until you're okay."

"Jim, get her out of here," Ellen said. "Go take her to your truck and get her home."

"But what about you?"

"Darce'll take me home."

I didn't care who took who home. I wanted to breathe.

The smell got stronger; it burned my eyes, probably sending tears clogged with mascara running down my cheeks, but I didn't care.

Jimmy lifted me upright, and I held onto him as he led me away. I heard someone say, "Is she all right?"

I couldn't see. My legs turned to jelly. That smell so strong, so sharp and then, as we walked out of carnival grounds and into the parking lot, it went away, but I didn't let go of Jimmy.

We kept going, past the parked cars, into the small grove of trees behind Darce's truck.

"I think I'm okay now." I stepped away from him and took a few big gulps of air to make sure. My breath caught in my throat. I pressed my hands against my eyes and tried to wipe away what had to be makeup caking around them and then stopped; it didn't matter.

"Thank you. I'm okay. You can go back to your date. I must have gotten a whiff of something bad." I looked at him. "I must have smelled betrayal."

"Betrayal?"

"Yeah, betrayal. You broke off our date so you could go out with Ellen. That's betrayal."

He shook his head.

"You got it wrong. I only did it because someone told me Darce was bragging about how easy it had been to get a date with you, and if you were easy in one way . . ." He looked away for a moment. "I just wanted to beat you canceling our date."

I leaned back against a tree and took off my sandals. My feet sank into the grass. It felt good to be standing barefoot on the ground. I let his words hang in the air for a few minutes. They made me feel like sinking lower.

"How come you never told me about applying for other jobs or your new house or anything? How come you told Ellen?"

"I've told you a couple things, but you don't listen except if I'm telling you about Darce. But I didn't tell you about how he still calls Ellen, begging her to go out with him again."

I didn't want to look at him and especially after he added, "I didn't think I had to warn you about him. Guess I was wrong."

"Oh." I bit my lips together and looked back toward carnival. I wondered what my dad would say when I walked home early and alone.

"Well, congratulations on the job and the house. Sorry for . . ." I looked toward him and then back at carnival. Somebody announced Kitty Wells followed by cheers from the crowd. It would be a long walk. "Sorry for tonight. Sorry for, for . . ." No point in apologizing further. He knew. "I guess I'd better go home. Think my night's over."

Jimmy grabbed my arm and spun me around.

"Fran, wait. You want to go out next Friday to help me celebrate?"

"Huh? You want to celebrate with me after tonight?"

He put his hands on my shoulders. I liked the feel of them there. "Fran, I've liked you for a long time, more than as a friend, even when you ask about Darce. Thought you knew that."

I bit my bottom lip and looked up at him.

"I didn't like seeing you with him tonight. You know how I won that teddy bear? I imagined throwing the basketball right at his face."

I laughed and thought about how I'd probably have won if I'd imagined Ellen's.

"So you want to go out on a real date?"

The air smelled good, like orange blossoms in a bridal bouquet. Kitty Wells sang *According to my Heart*. Carnival had started.

I inhaled. "Do you smell that?"

"You mean the smell of oranges?" He took a big sniff. "Is that your perfume? Nice." His hands came off my shoulders.

"I'm not sure."

"Oh." He stepped away. "Okay. Well, let me know if you want to go out."

"No, no, I'm not sure if it's my perfume. It's, well, yeah, yes, I'll go out with you next Friday, Jimmy. Jim. I want to go on a date with you, a real date."

Jim's hands came back on my shoulders, but just for a moment, because they moved down my back and pulled me into him. We stayed that way for a long time.

Later as I got ready for bed I looked for the perfume, but the strange red bottle was gone. Neither my mom or dad had seen it. I wondered if it had run back to the witchy old woman.

I went looking for her the following Friday at Mean Mike's, but the stand of half-used perfumes was gone, and Claire's stand was back.

When I told Claire about her, she said, "That's weird. I was told nobody was here last week."

I didn't say another thing, but I had a feeling that somewhere at another flea market, that old witchy woman was at her stand, selling a blood red bottle of half-used, strange, magical, wonderful perfume to some other gal.

A writer since fifth grade when her short play, My Last Countess *received an A,* ***Angela Binner*** *earned her MA in writing creative fiction from Seton Hill University. Writing is an enduring passion that keeps her working into the early morning. When not writing, Angela can be found reading or grading the papers of tomorrow's best sellers in the high school where she teaches ninth grade English.*

FERAL

by Lynne Reeder

Her skin radiates. That's part of the problem. It sings to me, and at night, it shines like the moon fell into her. I need to slide that skin from her bones, to savor it between my teeth, to pull her into me. Where she belongs.

She walks closer and I shrink into the shadows of the forest line. It's starting already, the familiar twist in my spine. My hands grow curved, each finger breaking into a claw with every step she takes. This happens every time I linger, but I insist on watching her pass by. I can't tear my eyes away. My heart quickens and the trees around me begin to blur. It's autumn, and the leaves flame all around my head. One falls into my vision just as she pauses. Her hair, red and blowing about her, breathes lavender, and I trace the tendrils tickling at the space between her collarbone and neck. My nose protrudes now, elongating into a snout, and she fills me. I ingest her air, the scent of purple circulating through my veins, erupting my blood vessels. I stoop, my back hunching and forcing me to all fours. The pain of transformation breaks from every pore, until I'm gray and bristling. I shake out my fur, making sure it's fully emerged.

She stoops too, but only to place her palm against the gravestone. Her fingers trace the shape of her grandmother's name, and her shoulders tense. The space around her has turned solid as stone, and suddenly indigo burns into my brain. I revel in her sadness. My eyes close and I inhale, strength flooding my muscles. My tongue starts salivating, and flashes of her flesh open before me. Her hair taunts me, cloaking her face, until she stands and turns toward where I hide.

Her eyes search for me. She knows I took the life from her grandmother's chest, ripped it away in strips. Because if she won't love me, then I'll take what she loves, make it a part of me, until she has no choice.

She returns to the path, the breeze playing havoc with my senses again. The moon is only a sliver tonight, but it doesn't matter. The change is complete. She moves away, but glances back once, flicking her locks over her shoulder like sparks of a fire. Had I not known any better, I'd have thought it was accidental. But she wanted to be sure her scent reached me still.

For you see, it's not the moon above that's fated me to this. It's her. She's why my lips curl into a snarl, why my fingernails turn to claws, why my skin buries beneath a thick mat of fur at the sight of hers. She still shimmers even as she descends down the hill that leads out of the woods, and it's magnetic. I slink along, keeping her in my vision, and I'm boiling now, because all I can see is her. My love. My hate. My fate.

My little red.

***

Before her, I'd grown in black and blue.

Once, when I was five, I'd taken a cookie from our kitchen without asking. When my father came in and glimpsed the crumbs still clinging to my lips and hands, he'd grabbed my wrist and leaned down, the ash of his cigarette hovering before my eyes.

"Did you steal from me, boy?"

I didn't exactly lie, because I'd been too scared to even utter a whisper. I stood there, silent, staring at his thumb digging into where my heart thudded beneath.

The ash flickered, and rained down upon my outstretched arm. My eyes never left that hand gripping me tight as handcuffs, not even after his other hand descended and the tip of his cigarette flamed against my skin. My father's attention would grow to feel like this, pressure and scars in formation.

Even at five, I knew I better not cry. I could feel his stare boring into me. He let the cigarette burn down to the filter before removing it.

"Let that be a lesson to you," he'd said, pushing me against the fridge. The bruise that circled my wrist lasted for a week. I still have the scar from the cigarette, a perfect circle, darker than all the rest of me, like a full moon in reverse. In human form, I've got matching blisters lining both forearms. When I shift, I'm missing patches of hair in every place a mark remains.

My father's was a heavy love, and the older I became, the more he learned to bruise me from the inside. When he began to have trouble eating and his breathing turned sporadic last summer, we sat in a doctor's office to hear the word "cancer" curl about our ears like hands around wrists. I felt trapped and relieved all at once. He'd have me in his clutches until the end, but now I knew there'd be an end. Years' worth of ashes collected about my shoulders, but I pictured the phoenixes from my novels. Rising, reborn.

Nights were the worst. They'd descend, and while everything else slowed down, my brain sped up. I'd lay there, suffocating in the quiet, until I thought I might break into a thousand small particles. I'd listen to the noise of my father's oxygen tank, the loudness of my mother's absence. I envied the freedom she'd given herself so many years ago when she'd walked out the door and just never returned. I used to watch that doorknob, trying not to blink in case it turned and she breezed back into my life. I think I'd have gone on this way, forever waiting.

But then, I met Adena.

I'd developed the habit of sneaking out after midnight, when I knew my father was fast asleep. I just needed the air around me to not be so stale, and I wanted to exist outside of those walls. I'd stride down the sidewalk toward the woods that lined the edge of our development. A path led partway up a small hill, then trickled into nothing more than a blanket of leaves and fallen pine needles. I'd hike through the darkened tree trunks with only the stars as guides. The farther I went, the more solid I felt.

One night, I veered from my normal trek and found myself by a stream. And there, in the middle of the water, stood a girl. She clutched rocks in her hands, her white dress clinging to her body. She rocked slightly in the current that broke about her knees. It had rained a lot recently, so the water gushed and formed miniature rapids, foaming and sputtering, yelling to the sky.

I watched her without her knowing as she slipped the rocks into pockets of her skirt. Her head dropped too, catching the light slinking through the canopy above us, and her hair ignited, the only spot of color in this muted place. She lowered herself the way a caterpillar creates a chrysalis, a process so methodical and beautiful I didn't realize what she was doing until her red locks hit the water, circling about her in the current, the final threads of silk closing over her head.

The water roared and the sound reminded me of my father and my feet wouldn't move. I stared at the spot where she'd stood. *She can't be drowning herself,* I thought. The water was only knee deep. But it was an angry stream, gushing over and swallowing her up. I wondered if rocks were hitting her face like fists, if more were working their way to clash against the ones she'd already nestled deep in her pockets.

Time melted away as I stared. It wasn't until her hand broke the surface, fingers outstretched like a butterfly wing unfolding, that I ran. The ground peeled away beneath my feet and I hit the water, the coldness of it sucking air from my lungs. I had no idea what to do next but I pushed forward, staggering toward the spot where her hand had been, until I hit something solid and my upper body pitched forward. The fabric of her dress caressed my calf. I plunged my arms into the water and struggled to get a hold of her before disinterring her from beneath. Water cascaded from her as I lifted her to the surface, a gentle rain to accompany the swelled tides and eddies all about us. Her arms hung at her sides, elbows like broken feathers.

I managed to drag her to the bank, where I collapsed. The world spun about me, my breath heaving from my chest. I dragged myself above her and stared at her mouth, slightly open, and noticed her stillness. I pressed my lips hard against hers and blew labored breaths into her.

I pushed against her chest, an instinct taking over, mimicking what I'd seen on television all those nights my father had been too busy or too drunk to do much more than flick on the set and growl out a warning about not making any noise. Lips, chest, lips, chest. Breathe, push, breathe, push.

She coughed, dark water spilling out, rolling onto her side, away from me. Her body convulsed, but I could only see the blades of her shoulders protruding like emerging wings. We stayed that way for so long that I began to wonder once again if this was really happening. The sky lightened around us, and she grew quiet, nothing left in her to hold her down. She lifted herself up and tilted her head skyward.

Without turning around, she said, "You want to tell me who you are, now that you pulled me back into this void?"

I curled my fingers into the forest floor, digging into pieces of leaves and twigs and churned up dirt. My voice came out scratchy, and I tossed it toward her though she was only a few feet away from me. "Rafe."

She turned to me. Her lips were close and I wanted to kiss her.

"Well, Rafe," she said, "I'm Adena. And I suppose it's nice to meet you."

Red hair, green eyes, pearly skin. She shimmered with the last of the water clinging to her surface. In school we'd read about sirens, enchanting creatures who lured sailors to their deaths with their beauty.

"Yeah," I said, sealing my fate. "It's nice to meet you too."

***

We became a secret. For a month, we snuck away and met by the water under the dark blue sky. And the more she revealed to me, the more I built her up in my mind. The more I trusted her.

We often laid beside the stream, heads touching as we watched the moon's phases above. Adena would stand to walk to the water's edge from time to time. She'd dip her toes and make small circles, watching them ripple out.

"My mother and father died when I was young," she told me during one of our secret rendezvous. She had this way of blurting out things. I knew to just wait, let the ripples of her mind expand out until she would be ready to say more. "I just wanted to see them again, really."

It was the most she'd ever said about the night I'd pulled her from the water. I stayed still, not wanting to disrupt what was unraveling from her.

She came to lay by me once again, and her hand grazed mine. "My grandmother raised me."

"It's just been me and my father long as I can remember," I told her. "He has cancer now."

"I'm sorry." Her fingers tightened their grip for the briefest moment.

"I'm not." The words sprung from my lips before I knew they were there.

A silence settled around us. "Sometimes," she said into my ear, so quietly it could have been the night air simply rustling my hair, "I wish my grandmother was gone."

I turned, and my eyes found hers. Our hands lay between us, a knot of knuckles and palms and secrets unleashed. Her mouth now only an inch from my own. When she spoke again, I could smell the hint of cinnamon on her breath. "I love her. I just want to be free." One breath, two. I waited. "Most of my life has revolved around keeping her happy. She needs me to do everything for her now. Cooking, cleaning, shopping. I go to school, I come home to care for her, I wake up in the middle of the night to guide her back to bed because she's forgotten where she is and who I am. Then I'm up early to do it all again the next day." She squeezes my hand, then points to the stars. "When she's gone, I'll have no one holding me back. Just wide open space."

Cinnamon swirled about me, and the softness of her lips found mine. And I knew then what she meant, how wonderful it would be to have nothing but this wide open space opening within us. I pressed into her, wondering if I'd ever feel as free as this night, this moment.

I still hold onto the fact that she was the one who kissed me. She pulled me in first. She broke me open with her words and her lips, her siren song that took me under before I truly knew what was forming deep inside my skin.

The night that changed us forever fell hard. My father had been stagnant, not getting any better, but also not getting worse. My days became a repetitious cycle of medicine, charting, changing sheets, prepping, calling, paying. He slept and breathed, and I listened. He woke and coughed and insulted, and I listened. He lived and I ached. And I listened.

The time the doctors had given him came and went and still he lingered. I could feel the hope sliding from my skin. Only the promise of Adena in the moonlight held me together.

The night I first changed began when my father threw his dinner across the kitchen floor. Spaghetti sauce splattered everywhere. I stared at the trail of red sliding down the table leg, dotting his oxygen tank and cord. Noodles stuck to the side of the fridge, and the plate rolled until it landed two inches from my feet.

"Clean that up." He coughed, a wet sound that dripped from his chest.

I bent down and picked up the plate. "Dad, you need to eat."

"Not that shit."

I clenched my jaw, tightening my grip on the plate. I put one noodle back on it, then another. "It's what we have."

He pointed to the fridge. "Just give me a beer."

"We don't have any."

"Like hell. Get me one."

"We don't have any, Dad. I'm not old enough to buy it for you."

"You backtalk—" He started coughing again, and the sound of it pounded against my temples. A vein jumped, my blood pulsing with every word.

"We talk about this every day." I picked another noodle off the floor, edged closer to the table. "You can't be drinking anyway. The doctors told you that."

"They also said I'd be dead by now."

"Yeah, well." I picked the noodles off the refrigerator door and threw the plate back in front of him.

He looked up at me and glared. The oxygen tank kicked on. He reached out to knock the plate down again but before he could, I grabbed his wrist. He felt so frail, so small. The blood was still pounding, my temples throbbing. The night settled in around the house, and I saw the moon sliding in around the edges of the kitchen window. He should have been done eating by that time, should have been climbing into his bed while I checked his tank levels and shut the bedroom door. I should have been locking him away and moving toward my freedom, my spot of light amidst the shadows.

He was keeping me from Adena.

And suddenly, I knew he'd always keep me from her. He'd infect this small happiness the way he'd always done.

He tried to pull away but couldn't. I'd become so much stronger than him. I pressed my fingertips into his wrist harder, not caring if it bruised. The old burn scars on my forearm glistened, the damaged skin almost igniting in the dusty light.

My foot stood inches from the oxygen tube. I shifted until it lay beneath my shoe. I pushed down, pinching it closed.

Adena's words pounded through my veins. *"I'll have no one holding me back. Just wide open space."* My father scratched at my face, feeble hands flailing before me. His lips moved, forming silent insults. They meant nothing. I'd already smelled the fear in his eyes.

The oxygen tank gasped and choked but not quickly enough. I pictured Adena looking for me, then leaving, impatient as the night dragged on.

With a swift motion I ripped the air hose in his nostrils toward the ceiling and grabbed the unused knife sitting on his placemat. His neck lay open before me like a sacrificial lamb.

Slitting his throat released me. Anger surged and the blood spilled, and the hotness of it enveloped me. I should have been appalled. But as he slumped before me, staining the beige kitchen tiles, the spaghetti still untouched before him, I felt more alive than ever before. I wiped at the river upon my face, dropping the knife beside the oxygen tank and turning to the door and my wide open spaces.

I ran toward Adena, adrenaline pumping through me. Just beneath my skin, my bones stirred. I wanted to burst into the woods, break off the boughs and branches and expose the entire sky above. The urge to howl rose in me and I tilted my head to the sky, ready to cut loose, when I came to the clearing and found her still there.

She turned at the sound of me. My eyes must have been wild and lit, though, because when she met my stare she shrunk away, stepping closer to the stream, one foot almost submerging in it.

The colors of the world shifted before me. The trees faded away, and Adena's veins seemed to pulsate. It was as if now that I'd experienced blood, I longed for more. My eyes narrowed at the cascade of brilliant red hanging about her shoulders. It was all the color I could see. I walked to her, aware of the pulsing in her throat.

"No."

The word shook me. Adena stood in the stream now, the water rushing about her knees, just like that night, that infinite night, when we began. Only this time she wasn't putting rocks in her pockets. She had one clutched in her fist, her hand raised toward me.

"Stay back, Rafe."

I laughed in disbelief, but it came out as a growl. I tilted my head at her, curious as to why she'd be afraid. Didn't she know there was nothing left to worry about, now that he was gone? I reached out to her. "Adena, you don't understand."

"I understand that's blood on your clothes."

My clothes. I'd completely forgotten about my clothes. I looked down and discovered dark brown stains splattered across my chest, my arms and legs. I became aware of the caked spots along my jawline pulling my skin tight. I wiped at them as if it was only dirt. I hadn't known blood was so permanent a mark.

"Adena, just—"

"I'm warning you."

"You need to—"

"What have you done?" she whispered. Her arm sagged. "My God, Rafe."

"I didn't do anything wrong." I stepped toward her but instantly her fist snapped back to attention. She was making me nervous. My skin itched with her fear. I held up my hands defensively. "It was him."

"Who?" Her eyes flared. Her hair fell over her cheekbone. I wanted to push it back, trace her lips.

"My father." I bristled at that word.

"What did he do?"

"It doesn't matter."

A sob escaped her. "What happened, Rafe?"

She poised herself like a rabbit ready to run from the approaching predator. I held out my hand. "I did what you said."

"What? What do you mean by that?"

My toes curled and uncurled and I hunched my shoulders, unable to keep from ramming my hands into my hair, holding my head. "Wide open spaces. Adena. Remember? You said—"

"Please, Rafe, don't say—"

"You said you wanted to be free."

"God, please—"

"So did I."

"You didn't—"

"I made myself free."

She folded in half, almost dropping the rock as her hand flew to cover her mouth. Her once glorious wings crumpled about her now. She crawled back to the safety of her cocoon. And that's when I knew what was wrong.

I had freed myself, but she was still trapped. Ensnared in the love and the obligation of her grandmother. She still had to worry over medical debt, dispense pills and change soiled sheets, live to safeguard a frail old woman who didn't even remember who she was anymore.

"Adena, I'm going to free you, too," I said and turned to follow the trail she traveled to reach this hideaway. I knew I'd be able to track it. Her lavender scent hung on the very leaves.

Her scream hit me before the rock did. I thudded to the ground, pain exploding around my brain. I felt a slow trickle begin down the back of my neck. Dirt caked its way into my eye. When the blood ran down my shoulder and dripped onto the forest floor, pooling in the puddle of moonlight, it ignited my bones. I began for the first time to curve and crack then, my spine protesting, my brain throbbing.

I focused on Adena as I struggled to stand, only to find I couldn't. My feet and hands seemed anchored to the ground. The blood dripped. My eyes watched hers. She didn't understand. She didn't understand. She didn't believe me.

A cloud shifted, and suddenly bright moonlight flooded across my body and floated in the pools of Adena's amber locks. I watched the way her red hair effervesced and remembered I'd left the lights on in my kitchen, the harsh bare bulb glaring over the red there too.

Then my body broke.

***

They never found me. My father's body was bagged and removed. From the edge of the woods I saw the yellow tape, the silent ambulance, the milling officers. They collected evidence and speculated theories and searched for the missing boy. And I listened. They came into the woods, found my bloody and ripped clothing by the river, shouted my name. And I listened. They stopped looking, and the investigation died out and I lived on. Still listening.

I remained in my wolf state for weeks that first time, getting my bearings, but always, always, tracking Adena. She'd unleashed what my father had inspired in me, and I still wanted to free her too. I thought, when I'd found her grandmother's house and let myself in the door, when I'd ripped at her throat and felt the familiar blanket of blood across my snout, she'd see. She'd understand. She'd have nothing holding her back and only me to run to. No one left to love but me. And so I thought she'd come back to our wide open space and blossom before me again, because she'd have nowhere else to go.

But not so. And now I'm here, watching her leave me again. I can't emerge from the woods. Once she's out of my sight I'll change, but I belong to the forest now. Since stealing her grandmother's life away, I've only transformed when she's near me again. Like those sailors in those storybooks, I'm forever drawn to her even knowing the way she destroys me. I'd once thought her to be a butterfly, but she's more. She's like a hawk with talons beneath human skin that only tear me apart when she's close by. And she does come near me still, every night. She visits the grave and I feel her resentment radiating from her and yet—she chose our clearing as the resting place. Perhaps love is a wild thing. Something dangerous we cannot keep from craving, something beyond human. Deep and innate, like the instinct to protect. And survive.

As she rounds the bend of the road like the stream breaking away from me, I tilt back my head to howl out to her, long and loud. Because this, I know she hears.

I know she waits and listens.

Lynne Reeder *earned her Master's in Creative Writing from Wilkes University and recently completed a year-long workshop on novel writing. She has had multiple short stories and poems published and currently holds the title of Poet Laureate for her hometown, all while being a passionate high school English teacher. When not writing or instructing, Lynne spends her time exercising her imagination with her five-year-old daughter, who is never at a loss for creating continuing plot twists. She resides with her daughter, husband, and pitbull in central Pennsylvania and looks forward to welcoming her second child in January.*

MURDER IN THE UPPER GALLERY

by Don Helin

I held open the door to the Berman Gallery for my wife, Delilah. Nearly six-feet tall, with a black ponytail and earrings that could pass for hula-hoops, she dominated any room she entered.

Delilah's heels clicked on the floor as she approached the receptionist, swinging diamond-studded sunglasses in her hand. "Mr. Chad Watson is here. His painting, *Thoughtful*, won Best of Show."

A young lady with dishwater blond hair and a name tag that read Amy, jumped up. "Oh, Mr. Watson, I'm in the Fine Arts program. You're my hero."

Amy bumped an end table, almost knocking over a lamp, as she hurried around the counter to grab a pamphlet. "The show's in the Upper Gallery. Mrs. Winter will be so-o-o upset that she missed you."

I forced a smile. "Thank you, Amy. Please give my regards to Mrs. Winter."

Delilah grabbed the program. "I'm going to find some coffee, darling. Don't forget, we agreed to meet Daddy for lunch."

Delilah was a trust-fund baby which meant that my Mercedes and monthly allowance were compliments of Daddy. Now don't get me wrong; I enjoy Delilah, but I delight in painting without worrying about money, and I adore my 230 SL.

"I'll be there shortly, my dear. I want to see the painting one more time."

Thoughtful held a place of honor inside the main entrance to the upper gallery. My model, Harmony, had jet-black hair and full red lips. Her nude body leaned forward, ice-blue eyes challenging all who entered the gallery.

Harmony had posed for my Thursday evening artist cooperative. When I wasn't able to finish the painting that night, I asked her to come to my studio. Fortunately, Delilah hadn't found out. If she did, I could kiss my Mercedes goodbye.

I stepped up on the last stair to the gallery and once again marveled at Harmony's beauty. As I stood looking at her nude body, a feeling of warmth spread through me. I watched, almost in a trance as she winked at me. I rubbed my eyes. Winked? That's impossible. She winked again. What the hell?

I glanced around to make sure no one watched me. Could I be losing my mind? No. Must be just my imagination.

I felt myself pulled forward toward the painting. Her lips formed a kiss, then her nude body leaned farther forward and her arms enveloped me. I could feel her naked skin against my arms, my cheek, my neck. The warmth. Damn. The warmth.

I shook my head and pulled back, quickly looking around. No one else here. I still felt the trace of her warm breath on my neck. My god, was I going nuts?

She laughed, that gentle tinkling laughter of hers, almost like chimes. I turned to look again down the stairs. Still no one around. Thankfully, no Delilah.

I looked back at the painting, wiped my brow and took a moment to cool down. This time Harmony stayed in the painting, no winking, no kisses.

Better get out of there before Delilah arrived. I hurried through the rest of the gallery to the back stairs. Thank god, no one saw me. What would they think? What would Delilah think? What did I think?

At the far corner of the gallery, the door to the janitor's closet stood partially open. A black high-heel shoe lay on the floor inside the door. That seemed odd, so I pushed open the door. The shoe lay next to a pair of legs that disappeared into a red dress that led up to a woman's face. A knife stuck out of her chest. Harmony's chest.

I had trouble breathing and bile rose in my throat. I grabbed at the knife, then realized I shouldn't touch anything.

Later I couldn't remember what I had yelled, but footsteps sounded. Amy appeared at the door, Delilah peering over her shoulder.

Delilah grabbed her cell phone, dialed 911. "I'm at the Berman Gallery. A woman has been attacked. Send the police and an ambulance right away. Yes, you fool, the Berman Gallery at Stanton University."

A hand touched my shoulder. Delilah whispered, "My poor baby. And you had to find her."

Delilah had no idea of my state of mind. Harmony, with those lovely red lips, lay dead on the floor. And had I just seen her? Touched her? Been kissed by her?

A uniformed police officer arrived, the point person in a platoon of blue—stretching yellow tape, snapping pictures, and measuring distances.

I ended up on a black leather couch in Mrs. Winter's office trying to figure out what had just happened.

The officer stood in the doorway. "I understand you discovered the body."

I had to steady my breathing. "That's right."

"Did you know the young woman?"

I didn't answer. All I could think of was Delilah's breath on my neck, her arm over my shoulder and Harmony laying on the floor upstairs. Or was she in that painting?

More footsteps. A man of about thirty-five, smartly dressed in a blue suit, white shirt, and red tie, appeared next to the officer. My face reflected in his tinted glasses. "I'm detective Myron Trefrey. Your name, please?"

"Chad Watson. This is my wife, Delilah."

"I understand you were the first one to see the body."

"That's right."

"Did you touch anything?"

Delilah came to my rescue. "Can't you see the poor baby is in shock?"

"I'm sure this is a shock, but we need to establish if Mr. Watson contaminated the crime scene in any way."

"Let me think. I saw a shoe on the floor through a crack in the door so I pushed the door open. There she was. I knelt down and felt for a pulse in her neck. I may have touched the knife."

"Did you know the deceased?"

Delilah's voice cracked like a rifle shot. "He didn't know her. Can't you ease up on him?"

"I'd like to hear from Mr. Watson."

"She modeled for my artist cooperative one time, but no, I didn't know her." I glanced up at Delilah. She nodded. Smiled.

Lieutenant Trefrey turned to Amy. "Did you know the deceased?"

"Yes, of course. Harmony Rogers is one of our most popular models."

"And your name is?"

"Amy Bradford. I work at the gallery. Ah, I took the liberty of calling Melody Leonard. She's Harmony's roommate."

"How well did you know Ms. Rogers?" Trefrey asked.

"We did a few things together." Amy stood on one foot, then the other, like a kid who had to go to the bathroom. "Bar hopping, a movie, you know."

Lieutenant Trefrey seemed to forget that I was there. Delilah's breath continued to tickle my neck. Maybe I could get out of this in one piece.

A rush of footsteps. "What happened? Is Harmony all right?"

A woman with dark hair and dressed in a trench coat, ran into the room. She had large round eyes, mascara tracks running down her cheeks. "I'm Harmony's roommate. Where is she?"

Trefrey led her toward a chair. "I'm sorry, but Ms. Rogers is dead."

The woman sagged into the chair.

Delilah jumped to her feet. "I'll get a glass of water."

In a moment or two the woman came around. "Thank you." She sat up and took a sip, her hand shaking. "Did you say that Harmony's dead?"

"I'm sorry, but yes. My name is Lieutenant Trefrey. Your name is?"

Pulling a tissue from her purse, she said, "Melody Leonard." She looked over as if seeing me for the first time. "Aren't you Chad Watson?"

Before I could answer, Delilah piped in, "Yes he is. What of it?"

Melody pointed her finger at me. "Why don't you ask him about Harmony? They had a thing going."

Trefrey turned toward me. "I thought you said you didn't know Ms. Rogers?"

Melody kept pointing at me. "He's an artist. Harmony told me she posed for him at a co-op, then he asked her to follow up with a special session at his studio where they got it on." She blew her nose again. "The bastard told her he loved her."

Delilah pulled back from me. "Tell them that's a bunch of crap. It is, isn't it?"

My mind froze. I couldn't speak.

Trefrey watched me. "Mr. Watson?"

"Yes, ah, I guess I remember now. She modeled at one of our co-op meetings. I asked her to pose one other time because I hadn't finished the painting. But, we didn't do anything else. I never really even talked to her."

Trefrey stared at me, as did the rest of the room. "Why didn't you tell me?"

Sweat popped out on my brow. "Lieutenant, I'm an artist. I probably have a hundred models pose for me each year. I can't know all of them. And how could I think straight after finding her on the floor like that?"

Melody's voice rose. "He's lying."

"Ms. Leonard, I'm going to ask you to step outside and wait until I finish."

Her voice echoed down the hallway. "He's lying, can't you see that?"

"Lieutenant?" Amy's voice floated out like on a breeze.

"Yes?"

"Harmony and I went out two nights ago. She confided that Melody had become insanely jealous of her.

Apparently the two of them were, well, you know. I guess Harmony liked to swing both ways."

Delilah stood. "That's enough. Come, Chad, we're leaving."

Lieutenant Trefrey held up his hand like a traffic stop. "I'm going to ask you to stay until we're finished upstairs and I get this straightened out."

Amy pointed down the hall. "The employee break room, they can go there."

When Delilah and I reached the room, I waited for the explosion. I didn't wait long.

"Now, what the hell is going on? Did you have an affair with that tramp?"

"No."

Delilah stared at me, squinting.

"No," I repeated. "Honey, I don't know why she said that. Harmony's a model, for Christ's sake."

Delilah's shoulders relaxed. She smiled again. "I didn't think so."

Trefrey arrived. "Mr. Watson, I'd like you to take a lie detector test."

I thought for a moment. "And if I refuse?"

"Why would you refuse?"

"I'm a nervous guy. What if I get a false reading?"

"Our evaluator is good. We don't get false readings."

The door opened, and a woman entered. "Oh, Mr. Watson, I can't believe this has happened. I rushed over. Now this."

She was a heavy woman of about medium height. Round spectacles enlarged her brown eyes making her look like an owl. The lines in her face gave her a well-lived-in look.

Trefrey stood. "And you are?"

"Oh, my goodness, I'm sorry. My name is Bertha Winter. I manage the gallery."

"I'm Lieutenant Trefrey. This is Mr. Chad Watson and his wife Delilah."

"Oh, I know who Mr. Watson is." She smiled at me. "Did I hear right that Harmony has died?"

"It appears she's been murdered," Trefrey replied. "Did you know the deceased?"

"Oh, yes, lovely girl, absolutely lovely. Harmony modeled for our art classes. Mr. Watson's painting of Harmony won best of show. She was very proud of that."

I could feel the noose tightening around my neck.

Mrs. Winter sat on a wooden chair. She removed her glasses and dabbed at her eyes with a tissue. "I understand it happened in the Upper Gallery."

"That's right," Trefrey replied.

"Well, there's a motion-activated security camera in that gallery. We've had thefts so I installed the system."

Trefrey leaned forward. "A security camera? Where's the tape?"

"The cameras sends the pictures to a digital recorder that's locked in that closet."

"Who has key?" Trefrey asked.

"Staff members have a key to the the closet. All my employees know how to operate the system."

Trefrey jiggled the door. "Can you open this please?"

"I'll get the key." Mrs. Winter left the room and returned to open the door.

Trefrey started into the closet.

"Let me do it, Lieutenant. The system was donated by one of our members and it's sensitive." She reached in, fiddled with the recorder, and pushed a button. "There."

A hissing sound filled the room, and gray speckles ran across the screen above the recorder. "My goodness," Mrs. Winter said, "it appears to have been erased."

"Let it run," Trefrey said.

The four of us watched the gray speckles for about five minutes. I sweated out what it would show. Me doing god knows what, standing at the painting like an idiot?

After another minute, I came on the screen. The tape showed me walking down the gallery hall, finding Harmony, and reaching down to check for a pulse. I did touch the knife. Thank god. No smooching in front of the painting.

"It appears that the key portion has been erased." Trefrey's face twitched. "Stewart, bring the rest of the group into the break room."

Melody walked in and glanced over at me, then looked away. Amy shuffled in, her tiny feet moving about a half inch at a time.

Lieutenant Trefrey cleared his throat. "I'm going to ask each of you to take a lie detector test. Just routine."

Melody pointed at me again. "Why? He did it."

I may have inadvertently ducked.

"Please sit down, Ms. Leonard. We have a recording that shows the Upper Gallery."

"That settles it," Melody exclaimed. "Let's watch it."

"A portion has been erased."

Amy looked up for the first time, the tissue still clasped in her right hand. "What? That's impossible."

"Someone familiar with the system erased it," Trefrey said.

"Mrs. Winter wasn't here." Amy thought for a moment. "I certainly didn't do it. That leaves Melody."

Lieutenant Trefrey's eyes widened. "Why Ms. Leonard?"

"She works here too, as did Harmony."

Melody glared at Amy, her lips pursed in a tight line. "I wasn't even here this morning."

Amy straightened her shoulders. "I saw you in the staff room earlier today. It surprised me you were here on your day off."

Trefrey held up his hand toward Amy. "Were you here, Ms. Leonard?"

Melody fidgeted with her watch. "I don't know what she's talking about."

"Where were you?" Trefrey asked.

I watched the verbal cross-fire, relieved not to be on the griddle.

"Home, doing chores," Melody replied. "Harmony wasn't very neat, so I had to clean up our apartment."

"Did anyone see you?"

"I don't believe so, Lieutenant."

"How come you didn't answer your cell?" Amy asked. "I got voice mail."

"I must have been outside dumping the trash."

Officer Stewart moved closer to Melody.

"Ms. Leonard and Mr. Watson, I'd like you both to take a lie detector test," Trefrey said. "In the meantime, I'll get our photo lab to clean up the tape. We should be able to retrieve enough images to see who went into that room before Mr. Watson."

Mrs. Winter shifted in her chair again, causing a loud squeak. "You'll be able to see what happened before Mr. Watson arrived?"

Trefrey nodded.

The tape was key to clearing me with the police as well as with Delilah. "How long will it take to clean it up?"

"Maybe a couple of hours."

"Why not wait until we see the images before I have to take the lie detector test?"

Trefrey thought for a moment. "Makes sense."

"Lieutenant, I've had enough of this. You're persecuting Chad and all he did was discover the body." Delilah pointed at Melody. "It's obvious she did it."

I nodded along with Delilah. I had done nothing wrong. Well, not murder.

Melody jumped out of her chair. "Who do you think you are? Your husband killed my friend. Don't blame it on me."

Lieutenant Trefrey raised his palms, like a boxing referee, to motion the two women apart. "We'll get this straightened out when we see the tape."

Amy put her face in her hands and started to cry.

Mrs. Winter put her arm around Amy's shoulder. "Please don't cry."

Delilah squeezed my hand. Tension filled the room. If I got out of this, I would never stray again.

"I loved her, but she treated me like dirt. Harmony told me she'd found someone new." Amy's sobbing increased. "I was just a piece of trash she had played with and would throw away."

"Did you erase the tape?" Lieutenant Trefrey asked.

Amy nodded.

"Did you stab Ms. Rogers?"

"I didn't mean to do it. She laughed at me. I had to stop the laughing."

Trefrey read her rights to Amy. "You'll have to come downtown with me."

Melody shuffled toward the door. "I'm sorry, Mr. Watson. I cared deeply for Harmony."

Trefrey glanced at me as he stood at the door. "Mr. Watson, you and your wife are free to go."

I helped Delilah to her feet. "I had no idea you could get images back after they've been erased."

Trefrey smiled. "You can't."

"Oh." I breathed a long sigh of relief. Memories of Harmony's soft breasts and thighs filled my mind. I turned to Delilah, "Let's go have lunch with your dad."

Delilah took my arm and leaned her head on my shoulder.

"Oh, Mr. Watson," Lieutenant Trefrey called. "I found this letter in the decease's purse. It's addressed to you. Feels like photos inside."

Delilah thrust out her hand. "Let me see that." She ripped the envelop open.

I heard that tinkling laughter again.

Using his experience from the military, including eight years in the Pentagon, ***Don Helin*** *published his first thriller,* Thy Kingdom Come*, in 2009. His second,* Devil's Den*, was selected as a finalist in the 2013 Indie Book Awards. His thriller, Secret Assault, was selected as the best Suspense/Thriller at the 2015 Indie Book Awards. Don's latest thriller, Angel's Revenge, was released in May. He is an active member of International Thriller Writers, Military Writers Society of America, Pennwriters, a statewide writers group in Pennsylvania, and is a mentor with the Mystery Writers of America. Contact Don at www.donhelin.com.*

LITTLE WHIRLPOOLS

by Carrie Jacobs

Carla leaned against the railing and looked down into the water. The freshly budding trees and brilliant blue sky were mirrored on its still surface. She heard the sliding glass door open behind her and quickly wiped her eyes.

Andy walked up behind her. "What's wrong?"

Toby, their golden retriever, panted and wound his way around their legs, insisting upon being included in the hug.

Carla laughed through the tears and scratched Toby's head. "Absolutely nothing. I'm just a little overwhelmed."

"And maybe a little sad?"

"Maybe a little." Their youngest had just gotten married, emptying out the last of their nest. "Mostly happy, though. I can't believe we finally got our house on the lake."

His warm breath tickled her neck as his strong arms circled her body. "Me, either. It's amazing, isn't it?"

She leaned back into his embrace and turned her face toward the warmth of the sun. "We've worked so long and so hard for this. I'm afraid I'm going to wake up tomorrow morning and be back in the city, getting ready for work."

Andy chuckled. "Soon enough, we'll forget all about the rat race and all that concrete and the noise and it'll feel like we've been here forever."

"I know you're right." She took a long breath, pulling the damp, clean smell deep into her lungs. "I can't believe how clear the water is. I can see the bottom of the lake from here."

"Check that out."

Carla shifted her gaze to where Andy pointed. Dozens of fish darted around. The surface rippled and swirled in their wake. "That's neat. What's over there? They look like little whirlpools." Away from the fish, five or six tiny swirls appeared and just as quickly were gone. A few seconds later, another set of little whirlpools broke the surface of the water and disappeared.

With a reluctant sigh, she gave Andy a quick kiss. "Let's finish unpacking these boxes."

"Why don't we take a break and walk to the diner? Get some food and relax a little bit?"

"I don't know. There's so much left to do . . ."

"The important stuff is already unpacked," he reminded her.

She only hesitated for a second. "Okay, you win."

"Wow, that was easy. Maybe this fresh country air will help me win a lot more often."

Carla elbowed him playfully. "Don't count on it, mister."

They strolled, hand in hand, down the dirt lane that connected their new piece of paradise to the rest of the secluded lake community. A modest three-bedroom bungalow on a two-acre sloping lot, it matched most of the other properties at this side of the lake, away from most of the summer tourists.

"You know this means we need to get a boat. And some jet skis. And a lot more fishing gear."

Carla rolled her eyes. "We *need* to get a working stove."

"That's what the diner's for."

Skinny's Diner, which clearly had not been named after the owner, boasted the best hot roast beef sandwich in the tri-state area. That night, however, the main dish on the menu was gossip. Every booth was full. An electric buzz of nervous energy pulsed through the room with the waves of hushed conversation.

Carla and Andy sat on the only vacant stools in the place. Their waitress leaned her hip against the counter with an exhausted sigh. "D'you need menus, or are you just here to swap tales like everybody else?"

Carla turned and asked, "What's going on, Grace?"

Grace lowered her voice. "You haven't heard? Joe Gabel beat Meg and the baby last night. Put 'em both in the hospital."

Carla gasped and covered her mouth. "That's horrible!"

"Ain't the first time with Meg, but the baby . . ." Grace shook her head. "Can't understand a man who'd knock a little girl down the stairs."

"At least he'll rot in jail."

Grace snorted. "Joe's a deputy and his daddy's in good with the DA. He's not getting anything but a stern talking to," she added bitterly.

The old man sitting beside her slammed his weathered fist on the counter, startling Carla. He leaned toward her, his eyes intense. "It's been five years. That's what's goin' on. Ain't got nothing to do with Joe Gabel," he growled.

Grace shushed him. "Come on, Earl, don't you be starting with that nonsense again." She refilled his coffee and rolled her eyes.

"I'm telling you, it's been five years. I knew it was coming, and if you all listened, you'd have known it, too." He drained his coffee. "Mark my words, Gracie, alla sudden, somebody's gonna disappear, just like Phil did."

Carla looked at Andy, who shrugged, just as clueless.

Grace filled them in. "Few years ago, Phil Waterson went out fishing and never came back. They found his boat and about three empty cases of Miller Light."

Earl turned on his stool and fixed his watery eyes on Carla. "*Five* years ago. They got Phil *five* years ago. *Every five years* when spring rolls in. There's *things* in that water."

Grace put her hand on her hip. "Sure, Earl, and I seen Bigfoot on my way in to work tonight. Don't be trying to scare people with that conspiracy theory nonsense."

He harrumphed and slammed a few dollar bills on the counter. "Tell me that in a few weeks. You'll see. They take one and they give one back." He stood, leaning heavily on his cane, and poked a thick, calloused finger in Grace's direction. "I'd rather you was right, Gracie, but you ain't." Earl limped out the door.

"Don't pay him no mind," she whispered.

Andy leaned his elbow on the counter and waited until the door swung closed behind the old man. "He seems pretty convinced. *Is* there something going on?"

"Earl . . . he's just . . ." Grace took a deep breath. "Look. Thousands of tourists come through here every year. People think they're fine going off the trails because they read a survival article on the internet. Or people—even the locals who ought to know better—get drunk out on the water. Well, sometimes people get hurt or go missing." She shook her head and swiped the counter with a damp towel. "Earl has a little too much time on his hands. Phil was his best friend, so somehow he put two and two together and come up with nine. Guess maybe it's easier than admitting Phil wasn't so bright."

***

Two months later, Carla sat at the end of their pier, her bare feet dangling off the side, above the water. The sun was hot, and the breeze over the lake felt wonderful. Her large floppy hat shaded her face from most of the rays while she relaxed.

The water rippled. Carla watched, fascinated, as tiny swirls formed on the surface. She leaned down a bit, fascinated by the little underwater cyclones. Hundreds of tiny . . . things . . . were swimming around, creating the little whirlpools. They looked like miniature bubbles, transparent but defined.

She sat back. Weird.

A bark startled her. She turned to find Toby running toward the pier, shaking like a leaf, growling. The hair along his spine stood straight up. Strings of slobber flung from his mouth in every direction as he barked. He stopped at the edge of the pier but refused to step onto it.

Goosebumps rose on Carla's arms. "Toby! What's the matter, boy?"

Terrified to think he might be having a stroke or seizure or any other horrible episode, she stood too quickly. A small gust of wind pulled the floppy hat from her head.

Without thinking, she reached out to grab it and lost her footing, tumbling off the pier and into the water.

Carla was an excellent swimmer, and she was only about twenty feet from the shore, maybe six feet from the ladder to the pier. But something was wrong. Very, very wrong. She had no buoyancy. No matter how hard she kicked and stroked, she couldn't stay near the surface. She held her breath, arms and legs flailing through gel, cold and slimy.

As Carla sank lower, her chest was on fire. She couldn't hold her breath much longer. Spots formed in her vision, her lungs desperate for air. It was impossible to hold her breath. She opened her mouth, and gel-water swirled in.

She heard Toby's frantic, desperate barks, then a splash. And then nothing. Her last coherent thought was, "Please don't drown. Andy couldn't take it."

***

Carla wasn't breathing, not exactly. She opened her eyes and looked around. Terror spiked through her chest, then she felt a needle slip into her neck and the anxiety drained away.

She could see the clouds and the sun, up through the clear water of the lake. She struggled to make sense of where she was. Judging from the position of the pier, the lake floor had to be just beneath her. Fish swam by, paying her no attention.

Carla felt like she was trapped in a clear box filled with slime. She could see out, up to the dock, to the bank, where people were running, pointing. Andy. Poor Andy, pacing, running his hand through his hair, helpless, with Toby by his side.

There were people in black suits. Divers. She let her eyes slide shut in relief. First one diver, then another, waded from the bank into the crystal clear water. There was no way they could miss her.

She waited, fighting to move the limbs she couldn't feel. Were they even still there? She struggled harder as the diver passed inches from her face. She swore his eyes looked directly into hers, but she knew in her heart, in her soul, that he never even saw her.

Carla tried to call out, but she couldn't move even her mouth. She imagined her brain sitting in a jar, unconnected to anything except her eyes. The second diver passed by, nearly as close as the first. He might as well have been a million miles away.

The divers left when the sun went down. If Carla had been able to, she would have wept. Instead, she just floated. Finally, Andy turned and walked away. Toby hesitated before tucking his tail and following Andy. Carla knew Toby knew she was right there.

The scene gradually changed, and it occurred to her that she was floating, skimming along the lake floor. Something bumped into her and changed the direction she was floating. She shifted her eyes, the only thing she could control.

She tried to scream, but couldn't open her mouth. Phil Waterson looked right at her, his bulging eyes nearly dead. His hair was gone, his face gaunt and skeletal.

A swarm of the bubble-things gracefully floated past Carla and came to rest on Phil. They covered his body and Carla watched in horrified fascination as the life was extinguished from his eyes, and whatever held him to the bottom of the lake let loose. Like a child letting go of a balloon, what was left of him floated straight to the surface.

The sun came up and went down again. The swarm returned and hovered above her. She studied the little creatures. They looked like stingrays, but transparent and no bigger than a dime. There were thousands, maybe millions of them, just milling about.

A few of them descended and Carla felt little pricks, but no pain. As she pondered this, she realized she didn't know if she was hot or cold. She couldn't feel anything other than those needle jabs, not even the beat of her heart, assuming it was still beating, or her breathing, if she was. Logic told her she had to be, but being trapped—alive—at the bottom of the lake suggested logic had no place here.

She lost count of how many times the sun rose and set. She alternated between praying for rescue, and praying for death. She was terrified of going mad, but saw little other option. She spent her days trying to recall every minute of her life with Andy. Her soul wept as she remembered the first moments she held her newborn babies: Drew, then Stefanie, then Maggie, then Dale. In her mind's eye, she saw Andy's face, oh, the pride on his face, when he held his babies, when he read them stories, when he tossed the baseball to the boys, when he had tea parties with the girls . . .

Months had gone by. Carla knew this because she saw snow flurries in the sky above the lake. Every few days, the creatures came to land on her body, their needle tails pricking her flesh. She had come to realize they were feeding. They slowly descended on her, so flat and depleted she could hardly see them. Then, after a few moments, they darted away, engorged and inflated, their outsides shimmery and healthy. She didn't even fear them anymore. She felt their collective consciousness and knew they meant no harm, but they needed to feed or die. Their only purpose was to exist.

Carla floated. She existed. She wished she didn't.

***

It was spring again. Ducks flew over the lake and sometimes paused in their journey north. The fish became more active. Carla watched them swimming overhead, oblivious to the world beneath the sand and grit they saw as the lake floor.

Carla had floated back near her home. She knew the creatures had made it possible when she caught a glimpse of Andy standing at the edge of the pier. He was so damn close. Carla saw his eyes, the deadness, the hopelessness. He was too thin.

"I love you," her mind screamed at him. "I love you, Andy, I love you!"

He stuffed his hands in the pockets of his jeans and blew out a hard breath, then he turned and walked away. Toby stayed tight against his leg. For that, Carla was grateful.

The pain on his face, the knowledge that he had no answers, no closure, ripped her apart. It would have been easier on him if she had been brutally murdered and dumped on their front lawn.

Instead, she was here, floating in hell, just fifteen feet away, and he had no idea.

***

It wasn't communication, not exactly. Carla knew things. She knew the creatures could sense her anxiety and emotional pain. When they felt it, they pricked her skin, releasing something that calmed her. She knew they claimed a new food source when the previous one was about to expire. Nothing personal. Just food.

Carla felt them, too. When they came to her hungry, she felt their emptiness, and their satisfaction when they left.

She thought about Earl at the diner.

They take one and they give one back.

He had been right. Mostly. Sometimes a person would last four years, sometimes six or even seven, depending on how long the creatures could harvest nutrients from the host before it died.

She floated. And she wondered if there was a way out.

Carla tried projecting her thoughts to the creatures. She would squeeze her eyes shut and create mental pictures. But nothing happened.

Until the trout.

Carla was staring up at a cloudless, perfect blue summer sky. A school of rainbow trout swam mere inches from her face, the colors dancing off their scales. She fixed her gaze on the fish as they darted around, blues, yellows, oranges, greens and reds catching the sun's rays and shimmering. She laughed, though only in her mind.

They swam past her in one direction, then shot off in another. Carla saw a school of the creatures corralling the trout into her line of vision. Were they doing this just for her? A wave of emotions washed over her. Gratitude. Relief.

Curiosity. And something she hadn't felt in the year she'd been at the bottom of the lake. Hope.

More days passed, blending into weeks. Carla experimented with the creatures. Slimy tendrils of seaweed swaying on the current obstructed her view, which irritated her. She hated not being able to see. She focused on the emotion until a swarm of creatures came and gently bumped her away from the plants.

A boat overhead blocked the sun. Annoyed, Carla stewed until the creatures shifted her position. From her new vantage point, the sun warmed her face.

There were no fishing lures dangling off the side of the boat, no line catching the waning sun. It was a small boat, barely larger than a kayak. Carla watched until she saw a face peering down into the water. Meg Gable let her fingers trail over the side, making ripples in the lake. She was smiling. Carla wished she could smile back.

A beer can plopped into the water, and Meg's expression turned to annoyance. She sat up, leaving Carla to stare at the back of her head. Meg's hands were animated, pointing at the beer can and gesturing in obvious frustration.

Then, the hand. An open hand, attached to a large, hairy arm, raised high and swung downward. The boat rocked heavily. Carla could only imagine the scene above the water until Joe Gable rose up from his seat, unsteady, his face contorted with rage. She couldn't see Meg.

Anxiety spiked through Carla. The creatures swam to her, but she didn't want to be medicated. She wanted to see, wanted to feel, even if there was nothing she could do. They seemed to understand, and let her be.

Joe raised his hand again, this time to pop the top on a can. He chugged the contents, then threw the can into the water. He leaned forward, his mouth open wide, undoubtedly screaming obscenities. He bent, swaying the boat again, and straightened, holding another can. He popped the top, chugged, and threw the can into the water, smirking.

Carla's vision narrowed, colored by anger and disgust. Surprise widened her eyes as Meg stood, holding an oar aloft. Her shoulders shook. Whether she was crying or screaming, Carla couldn't tell. Joe's mouth formed a perfect "O" as Meg swung the oar.

The water shook all the way to the bottom, rocking Carla. Joe floated calmly on the surface, facing the sky, his arms outstretched, a thin stream of red trailing in the water next to his head. Meg kicked her legs, sending the contents of a picnic basket bobbing in all different directions. Carla watched, fascinated, then confused, as Meg ignored the overturned boat and swam for the opposite shore.

After a few long minutes, Joe's fingers twitched and he began to sink. Then his arms flailed. He swam awkwardly, lurching toward the boat. He finally caught the edge and held it, his legs treading water.

***

Carla's mind raced. At this point she had nothing to lose, and everything to gain. If only the creatures would understand her. She projected anger toward Joe's dangling legs. And then, hunger. The creatures hovered nearby, not responding. She forced herself to stay calm and tried again. She imagined the old gnawing sensation in her stomach when she'd gone too long without eating.

A few stray creatures floated toward her, flat and empty. She focused on Joe, the bare flesh of his legs. The creatures paused by her, then a swarm shot upward, swirling toward him.

Carla closed her eyes. As much as she despised Joe Gable, as much as she was desperate to escape, she couldn't watch the terror she knew was on his face as he sank to the bottom of the lake. She couldn't afford any sympathy for Joe. Not if the creatures would accept him in her place.

When she opened her eyes and oriented herself, she stared up at her dock and let herself feel what she'd tried for months to suppress.

Homesick.

Longing.

Love.

The creatures darted away, leaving her. She felt awkward, knowing Joe was floating somewhere close by, likely terrified and confused. The sky turned dark, and she wondered if Meg had gotten home.

The boat floated away overnight, leaving a clear view of another beautiful blue sky. A mass of the creatures returned and swarmed around her head. They nudged her toward the shore, then, without warning, whatever tethered her to the bottom of the lake let go and she floated straight to the surface.

Carla crawled onto land, her muscles weak and nearly worthless. She vomited gel from her mouth and her nose, her stomach spasming. She retched and convulsed until the gel finally stopped spewing out. She greedily gulped air into her lungs. It felt like heaven and fire. She lay on the ground, shivering and soaked and overwhelmed by the instant return of sound, smell, taste, and touch. Everything was a frightening combination of ecstasy and pain.

Somewhere above her, she heard Toby howl, long, loud and insistent. A moment later, she heard Andy scream. No words, just some primal battle cry from his soul as he flew across the grass, falling and sliding and crying and stumbling and finally crawling to her side.

He gently cradled her in his arms, sobbing. Carla's fingers clutched his shirt, and she lost consciousness.

***

Carla stood at the end of the pier one last time, staring down into little whirlpools in the water. She hated to leave, but Andy couldn't live with the memories.

"Are you ready?" He seemed reluctant to disturb her.

"Almost," she answered with a smile.

Toby was watching them from the deck, but his tail was wagging.

"Do you think they'll ever find Joe Gabel?" Andy asked, taking her hand as they walked to the car.

Carla felt the faintest tinge of guilt. She thought maybe it should have been harder to trade another human being's life for her own. Then she pulled the sweet smell of freshly mowed grass into her lungs and squeezed the hand of the man she loved. "I'm sure he'll turn up eventually."

Carrie Jacobs *began her writing career at age three, by dictating a riveting tale to her transcriptionist (AKA her Mom). "A Frog Named Tog" rocketed to #1 in the family. Since then, Carrie spent fifteen years as a local newspaper columnist, and frequently writes articles for a local non-profit. She lives in central Pennsylvania with her husband Scott, son Austin, and their spoiled pets. You can find her online on Facebook at facebook.com/writercarriejacobs, on Twitter @carrieinpa, or on her website at carrieajacobs.com.*

ANGEL IN THE MIST

by Laurie J. Edwards

Annie O'Brien hurried along the gangplank, hunger and fear clawing at her belly. A solid wall of wood towered before her, gleaming in the sunlight. How could such a huge steamer stay afloat, especially once the crowd, shuffling along behind her, boarded?

Yesterday this long-awaited trip to America had seemed an exciting dream. She still couldn't believe she, of all her eight siblings, had been chosen to go. But Annie had no need to pinch herself to be sure; her younger brother Seamus had administered a swift kick to her ankle, which still smarted. Now this morning's tiny ration of cornmeal mush curdled in her stomach, and thoughts of Seamus filled her with homesickness.

When she reached the deck, the freshening breeze stung her cheeks and snapped the flags against the poles overhead, jingling iron rings on the ropes holding them aloft. The clanging metal reminded her of gaol gates slamming shut, caging her inside a prison. Drawing in a ragged breath, she struggled to still the quivering that shook her body as they lifted anchor and steamed out to sea.

Suddenly, being a housemaid in America did not seem a wonderful future. Annie longed to lay her head on Mam's aproned lap, to feel the work-roughened hands stroking her hair. What if she never saw Mam or Da again? America was so far away. She tried to comfort herself that all the money she earned would buy food to keep her family alive. The shriveled, blackened potatoes could not. Baby Norah had died of hunger in Mam's arms. Old folks, like Gran, hands gnarled, bodies hunched, lay curled on pallets in low-roofed cottages awaiting death. And she, Annie, was to be their savior. She would work hard, send her pay back to feed first her family and later the village. Grandiose dreams, yes, but Annie had a mission. And succeed at it she would.

As the gulf grew between ship and land, the emerald grass of her beloved Ireland hazed into the distance in a blur of tears. Annie imprinted every detail of the coastline on her heart. She clutched the rail, straining to make out the sliver of shoreline on the horizon. When not a speck remained, she stumbled below deck to find her bunk.

Never had Annie glimpsed such a room. The ceiling rose higher than the thatched roof of her house, and beds were stacked one above the other. If Annie stood with arms outstretched, she could touch both sets of bunks.

The first few women to enter spoke only in whispers, and the silence hurt Annie's ears. The ship shuddering under her feet seemed a poor substitute for the laughing and squabbling of her brothers and sisters. Shortly, though, the room filled with mothers of squalling infants and whining toddlers, making Annie feel more at home. But that night, tucked under the coarse woolen blanket, Annie fought sleep, fearing she'd crash to the floor as the ship dipped and rolled.

***

After breakfast Annie stood on deck, gazing back toward home. Then she strained forward to catch a glimpse of her future.

A shout startled her from her reveries. A red-faced girl holding a baby chased a runaway boy. The wiry, freckle-faced boy barreled into Annie, who caught him and twirled him around the way she did her younger brothers. He squealed and begged her to do it again.

"Thank you for catching him." The girl, not much older than Annie herself, puffed out a breath as she reached them. "I'm Frieda, the Luddingtons' nanny." The baby she balanced on her hip stared somberly from one to the other.

The boy muscled his way between them. “She’s not our real nanny,” he informed Annie. “Papa only hired her to take care of us ’til we get back to New York. Bridget couldn’t come on this trip. She had to stay home on Long Island with Mama when we went to London.” With his hands clasped behind his back as if he were a connoisseur studying a painting, he examined Annie. “I’m Joseph Luddington the Third. Who are you?”

“Joseph,” Frieda snapped, “mind your manners.”

Annie hid her smile at the young boy’s aristocratic manner and made a mock curtsey. “Annie O’Brien, at your service.”

“You have red curls like our Bridget,” Joseph said. “Maybe Mama would hire you too.”

Annie smiled. “I already have a job. The Duvalls paid my passage, so I must work for them.” When Joseph’s brows drew together, she added, “Perhaps later I could come to live with you.”

Joseph studied her a moment longer. “Do you play marbles?”

“Sure, and don’t I play with my brothers?” Not often. Chores usually took up most of the day, but she could shoot with the best of them.

Joseph took her hand and led her to a stateroom larger and more splendid than the chapel in her village. Two poodles raced toward them yipping. Joseph hugged each in turn. He dismissed Annie’s exclamations with a wave of his hand. “My daddy’s very ’portant. He went to England to ’stablish a new bank.”

They sat crosslegged beside the marble sunburst on the foyer floor. Annie, who had only ever played with gray clay pellets, stared open-mouthed as Joseph poured a swirl of rainbow-colored glass from a leather pouch. But as she often did with her younger brothers, she let him beat her occasionally.

***

A splintering crash followed by a clanging bell startled Annie from sleep. Feet pounded up the stairs on the other side of the wall. Doors slammed. Screams and shouts echoed in the metal passageway. Clad only in her sleep shift and clutching her reticule, Annie struggled down from her upper berth as the ship floor lurched first one way, then the other. Hanging tightly to the handrail, she pulled herself up the stairs after the stampeding crowd.

A man seized Annie as she rushed onto the deck. He shoved her through the crowd. "Here's another young one."

Rough hands grabbed her and pushed her right arm into a boxy cork vest. Her reticule dropped to the deck when a man grabbed the other side of the life vest and thrust her left arm through the hole. Annie's stomach roiled, and she shivered in the wintery air.

She sucked in a breath so she wouldn't cry out as a deckhand held her over the side. Waves lapped against the hull, sending the lifeboat below bobbing. What if she missed and went plunging into the ocean?

A baby's cry startled her. Annie looked over her shoulder. The nanny, clutching baby Sarah to her chest, hustled Joseph along. "Please," she pleaded, "let us through."

"It's too late. This boat is full. One more person could sink it."

The nanny's voice shrilled in fear, "The next one then."

"That's the last one, miss," the cabin boy's tone was somber. "Ain't no more."

Frieda's scream pierced through Annie. She looked deeply into the boy's eyes. Joseph—the one she'd played marbles with yesterday. And the baby. What if it were Seamus and Norah?

"Wait!" Annie struggled with the strings holding the vest together. Each second counted, yet her fingers fumbled. The boy needed a vest, and this was the only one.

"Stop!" The man who held her aloft shook her hard. "What are you doing?"

The stern of the steamer tilted deeper into the water. Passengers stumbled. Some fell. The man holding Annie slammed against the railing. Her feet dangled over it, her body swaying. The contents of her stomach crested and sank with each wave that battered the ship. Still, she tore at the fastenings.

"Give it to him." Annie pointed to Joseph. "He and the baby can take my place. They don't weigh as much as I do."

"Hurry!" The man set her on her feet and snatched at her loosened vest.

The nanny pushed Joseph toward them. He stood stoically while they adjusted the vest around him, his gaze fixed on Annie.

Annie scrambled on the floor for her reticule so he wouldn't see the sobs that threatened to overwhelm her. She groped through her purse for the postcard she'd addressed to Mam and Da. She reached over and shoved it into Joseph's chubby fist. "Send it to my mam, my family," she pleaded, "and tell them . . ." She choked back a cry as the crew lowered Joseph into the place that would have been hers. She bent over the railing and prayed that her words would not be lost in the wind. "Give them my love."

A sailor elbowed past her and shinnied partway down the rope, baby Sarah tucked into the crook of one arm. He tossed the toddler toward waiting hands. After a woman clutched Sarah close, the sailor let go of the rope and plunged into the sea. He reappeared, head bobbing as he stroked through the waves toward a fallen mast.

Tears rained down Annie's cheeks. Mam and Da. She'd never see them again. But Mam would understand.

Frieda clutched Annie's hand as the small ship rowed out of sight. "Bless you, miss."

They remained hand in hand as the liner groaned and creaked under their feet. The stern tilted, and the ship sank deeper into the waves.

***

All through the night, Joseph clutched the postcard. Water splashed into the lifeboat, dissolving the edges of the thin cardboard. Whenever he awoke, Annie's sorrow-filled eyes stared at him. When he slept, he dreamed of her.

For almost two days, the boat drifted on calm seas. The chilly night air bit through his damp sailor suit. People in the lifeboat huddled together in small groups for warmth and comfort, careful not to tip the boat. His lips cracked and swollen, Joseph slipped the postcard under his thigh. He cupped his hands to sip from the puddle on the floor of the lifeboat.

A woman smacked his hands, causing the precious water to dribble down the front of his shirt. "It'll kill ye, lad, for sure."

How could water kill him? Perhaps she only wanted to save it for herself. He was so thirsty. The sky and waves blended into one shimmering mass that stung his eyes and made him dizzy. Some people sprawled on the floor of the boat, others leaned back, eyes closed, their sunken eyes corpselike. Even shouts of a rescue ship barely shook Joseph from his stupor. He snatched up the postcard, toddled a few unsteady steps, and collapsed into the arms of a rescuer.

***

Joseph Luddington III stood beside his mother as his father's casket was lowered into the ground. Then Uncle Clyde supported his mother to the carriage, where the coachman opened the door. Heavy veiling trailed from her large black hat, hiding her face from view. When she reached for Joseph's hand, he quickly transferred the scrap of paper to his other fist. Then he clasped his mother's hand and, with a boost from the coachman, climbed onto the padded leather seat beside her.

In the trees at the edge of the cemetery, a girl stood watch, her red hair the brightest memory of that night. Joseph uncurled his hand slightly so she could see the tattered postcard before the coachman shut the door.

He was still fingering the postcard when they entered the house.

"What is that?" His mother's sharp voice startled him. "Throw away that filthy paper." She tried to snatch it from his hand, but Joseph squeezed it into his palm.

"You have no idea what kind of diseases it may carry."

Mama called for Bridget, who pried his fingers open. Bridget tossed the scrap into the fireplace. The postcard fluttered to the back of the stack of crumpled papers on the hearth.

Across the room, her body as transparent as smoke, the girl hovered over the hearth, glancing first at the scrap and then at him. Joseph squirmed. Surely she could see he'd had no choice.

After Bridget tucked him in bed, Joseph lay still, pretending to sleep. He forced his chest into a slow up-and-down motion. When Bridget retired to her room adjoining the nursery, Joseph tiptoed to the hearth and tried to spear the cardboard with the poker, but only succeeded in burying it under the ashes.

A breath on his cheek made him jump back. The girl caught the poker before it clattered onto the brick. She returned it to its place. Then she bent and scooped up the postcard. She blew the dust off it and handed it to him. He padded to his room and secreted the cardboard in his toy box. He'd made a promise that night, and he'd keep it.

That postcard was the only thing he had left from the ship. Everything else was gone. They'd forced him to leave it all behind. His toys, his dogs, his papa.

The girl's eyes haunted him. Night after night she came to him, begging him to help her family.

Several months later, when his mother had gone to take the waters and Bridget had her half day, Joseph told the cook, who had been charged with watching him, that he would join the coachman in the stable. In one fist he clutched his pocket money, in the other, the paper he had unearthed from his toy box.

Joseph cleared his throat. He tried to imitate his father's commanding tone. "I must go to Papa's bank today. I have some business to attend to."

The coachman gave a half bow and hooked up the horses. On the way to town, Joseph sat stiff and straight beside the coachman as the horses plodded along the streets.

Again, he used Papa as an example when they pulled outside the bank. "I won't be long."

Joseph entered the bank where he had often accompanied his father, and several tellers greeted him. He went to the cage and reached up to set his pocket money on the counter.

"So sorry for your loss, son. Your papa was a good man and is greatly missed." The teller counted the money. "Did you wish to deposit this in your account, Master Luddington?"

Tears stung Joseph's eyes as he stood on tiptoe to push the tattered cardboard across the marble shelf. "Send it to that address." Then remembering his manners, he added, "please."

The teller pursed his lips as he picked up the worn scrap. A frown creased his brow. "And shall I discard this then?" He pinched the cardboard between the tips of his fingers as if it might soil his hands.

Joseph gasped. "Oh, no. I need it."

That night the girl smiled at him, and the constant weight crushing his chest lifted. From then on, he made regular trips to the bank with his pocket money whenever Mama was away. Sometimes the girl floated along beside him when he walked, but he had to take care not to speak with her when others were watching.

If no one was around, she told him tales of her family. Her da's hearty laugh and the smoke curling from his pipe, her mam stooped over the heavy soup pot that bubbled over the fire. Her younger brothers tumbling together like a den of cubs, the older ones exhausted and blackened by coal dust. Mam and her married sisters hunched in the garden, digging up one shriveled blackened potato after another, cutting out the few useable bits to toss in the soup pot. Most nights the watery broth contained less than a handful of greens, potatoes, and meat. Sometimes only grass floated on its surface. Eight people sat down to a meal that would barely feed a small child, with little but charity cornmeal to plug the hollowness the rest of the day.

Each night as Joseph drifted off to sleep, lines of people with bloated bellies and sunken eyes, bones poking sharp angles under parchment-thin skin, empty bowls outstretched, crowded his dreams. They disappeared only on the nights he sent his pocket money to the address on the postcard.

***

When he turned eighteen, Joseph came into his trust fund. After leaving the lawyer's office, he booked passage on a ship sailing to County Mayo. The strange mewling his mother made when he told her reminded him of an animal in pain. Joseph almost gave in and promised to stay. But the girl appeared, staring at him with somber eyes.

"I'm going. I'm going," he assured her, waving the scrap of paper so she could see it.

His mother buried her face in a lace handkerchief, her shoulders heaving. Joseph laid one hand on Mama's shoulder and squeezed, then turned and walked away before her heart-rending sobs changed his resolve. He remained brave until he reached the gangplank.

Memories of his last walk up this slope tightened his throat so that he could barely swallow. Moisture clouded his vision as he returned to the tangled forest of trousered legs and billowing skirts of years ago. He'd clung tightly to Papa's hand but leapt up and down to see the water. The same waves now slapping the boat made his stomach churn, his muscles tense. He stumbled back a few steps, but the press of people waiting to board hemmed him in. Panic constricted his chest, making each breath painful.

And then she stood before him, trembling. He reached out and drew her toward him. He clasped her cold hand in his own sweaty one while they boarded and then led her to his cabin. People around him shrank back, whispered behind his back as he passed. But he cared nothing for their opinions.

In the cabin, they huddled together on the edge of the bed as the whistle blew and the ship shuddered. Once the liner steamed away from the shore, she slipped from his arms. Her outline grew fainter.

The panic that had engulfed him as the ship left the dock could not compare to the terror of losing her. "Don't go." He grabbed for her, but his hands slid through empty air. "I can't make this trip alone."

"You must." She hovered a few feet from the ground, then swooped down, and touched icy lips his cheek. "I'll see you on the other side."

Joseph pressed his fingers to the chilled spot, trying to hold the moment in his heart. Before him, she shimmered and dissolved.

To stem the tide of loneliness and fear, during the day he wrote feverishly. Each night he stood on deck, staring out to sea, one hand caressing the side of a lifeboat, pleading for her return.

As the ship neared the coast of Ireland, the seas whipped up a storm. Gale-force winds snatched his breath, blew him across the deck, and pinned him to the rail. Metal pressed into his gut as waves rose higher, splashing his trousers, his coat. Frigid water soaked through the wool until it clung to his skin, setting him shivering.

The next wave slapped him in the face. It left him gasping for air, a coating of brine on his tongue. Afraid to let go lest he slide across the deck into the sea, Joseph clenched the rail as the boat rose on the swells, then slammed into the troughs. Water poured over the sides, dragging him with its relentless pull. He came up spluttering after each onslaught, clinging to the rail. Then an anvil of water hammered against his chest, engulfing him. A white flash exploded around him. Water gurgled into his lungs, and he lost his grip on the rail. A dark liquid tunnel sucked him into the depths of the sea.

Annie came to him then, hands outstretched to greet him.

***

Three weeks later a trunk arrived in County Mayo. Inside a tattered scrap of cardboard bore the cottage's address. Under that lay stacks of paper. The scribbled story of Annie and the two lives she'd saved so long ago. Below that, tied in oilcloth, a will signed by Joseph Luddington III, leaving his entire trust fund to the family of Annie O'Brien.

On the hillside above that village now stands a carved marble statue of two angels, hands entwined, facing out to sea.

Laurie J. Edwards *is the founder of Leap Books, a publisher for twins and teens. She has worked as a freelance editor and is the author and/or illustrator of more than 20 published books for adults and children.*

PETRUS OF *ALDRINTOWN*

by Tom Galvin

"*Fence!*"

Two teenaged fencers lunged at each other. They danced back and forth, thrusting and parrying in a tin-ting of metal. Two coaches stood by, eyes fixed on the combatants.

A sensor on Michael' mask—the larger fencer—emitted a light, signaling he had been hit. He groaned and swung his arm down in disgust. A floating holograph above the piste hovered over the coaches' heads. It displayed two numbers—a red "6" and a blue "7" that changed to "8."

One coach whispered to the other, "He's got him."

The other said, "Almost. . . . All right, next point! . . . Positions! . . . . . . *Fence!*"

Within seconds, Petrus—the smaller fencer—calmly parried an errant lunge, and thwacked Michael on the collar bone. The "8" became "9" and flashed.

The fencers saluted. Michael, the loser, tore off his mask and walked away rubbing his forehead. Petrus slowly brought both hands to his mask, dropping his sword to the floor.

The coaches approached. "Well done, Petrus," they said, clapping. "You made the team!"

Petrus removed his mask, exposing wide brown eyes over a gaping mouth. The *team*. He raked one hand through his dark curly hair. First-years normally didn't make it this far. He trembled as he returned the coaches' handshakes. Other club members came forward, patting and hugging him. Petrus smiled back but could not muster words.

Petrus was not a clan member. His tunic was forest green, the color of the space mining city of *Aldrintown*. He was a municipal, the son of city workers, and the only municipal in the fencing club.

There was Captain Jeremy in a mustard yellow tunic, the color of his mining clan. The twins were clothed in copper red, and Michael—now the alternate, sported charcoal gray.

The *team*. Petrus could not stop bouncing on his toes.

The fivesome headed toward the residential decks. The corridors lined with Screens, wall holographs that kept the denizens informed. The South Astra Junior Olympics was three days away! The words replicated down the hall like dominoes followed by images of past *Aldrintown* medalists.

Petrus stopped at the nearest Screen. Congratulations to our Junior Olympians, it said. A picture appeared of The Badminton Team, eight boys and girls in white uniforms trimmed in forest green with the city crest and Olympics five-ring logo over the left breast. Next was The Track Team with its twenty-four members. And then, The Fencing Team. The foursome was shown for all in the city to see. Jeremy, the twins, and Petrus.

The *team*. Petrus surveyed his picture. *That's me?* The previous year, wearing that uniform was but a dream. He had joined his fellow schoolmates in the annual ritual, watching as *Aldrintown*'s Olympians paraded around the city in those bright outfits before boarding spaceships to travel far away and compete. He showed up because he had to.

But then he heard the announcement, that *Aldrintown* would be the next host. He thought, *Really? They would all come here?* He followed the Games, even though *Aldrintown*, as usual, won few medals. He fell in love with the spirit, the color, and the pageantry. He wanted to be a part of it. But until this day, he didn't believe he would actually compete. He thought it would be two more years, then maybe he'd have a chance.

He couldn't wait to tell his parents.

***

Petrus reached the stairs heading to the lowest residential deck. An exterior window resided at each landing. Petrus loved to stop and look out the one nearest his family apartment.

Four hundred kilometers below the orbiting city lay the aptly-named planet Greystone. It was night, allowing Petrus a clear view of five tiny clusters of lights spread far apart on the surface. Their relative positions told him whose mines they were: Jeremy's clan Scheemite in the center, the twins' clan Orwell to the left, Michael's clan Flettern to the right, with Mallian and Rockwell on the horizon.

Petrus wondered which mine his father was down there visiting. His father was a municipal power engineer, who occasionally traveled to the planet's surface to help the miners. The mining clans did not trust most municipals, but Petrus' father was an exception. They depended on him for their heat, light, communications, and air systems.

Petrus imagined giving the good news in person, but he could only send a message. There was no way his father could come back in time to see the Olympics. He put his hand on the window and hoped everything was okay down there.

Exiting the stairs, he navigated the maze of corridors leading to the apartment, finding the door locked. He sighed. Once again, his mother, a food, water, and waste engineer, was out late fixing something in the city.

Petrus flung his bag to the floor. A Screen lit one wall. An envelope icon flashed at the bottom, meaning a message was waiting in the inbox. At Petrus' gesture, the Screen opened a video message. There stood his mom, a woman of taut white skin and frazzled blonde hair, donning a bodysuit stained with oil and sweat. In one breath, she said, "Hey, I just saw your picture! You made it, eh? I can't believe it! Congratulations, I'm so proud of you. I'll try to get home as soon as I can. I sent a note to your father, too. Gotta go. Bye!"

He shook his head. He knew the message meant she wouldn't be home anytime soon. He served himself a dinner of standard white mush in an edible bowl and spoon, and instructed the Screen to open the Newsfeed.

Before long, the Screen turned black. A message appeared announcing the names of two miners earlier in the day. Their images appeared; both wore the charcoal gray uniform of the Flettern Clan.

He gasped when he saw Harland's image.

Harland recruited Petrus to the fencing club when he visited the school one day. Petrus was mesmerized by Harland's bronze medal, which his team won four years earlier. Then, he felt a rush as Harland took a fencer's position—face stern, standing on his toes, sword hand outstretched, offhand arched over his head. He spoke sweetly about the beauty and grace of the sport as he hopped on his toes back and forth, occasionally moving his wrist but otherwise holding his body perfectly in position.

The kids laughed, but Petrus was awestruck. Soon, Petrus would hold a real sword in his own hand.

Those first classes, the coaches told him he was a natural, but Petrus was so nervous, he struggled to hold on to the sword, and every part of body ached for hours afterward. But Harland took an interest in Petrus, constantly telling him to, "Just relax."

Weeks later, after Petrus had mastered the basic, Harland was gone. The Fletterns sent him down to the mines. He dutifully obeyed. Petrus would never hear from him again.

He turned off the feed and abandoned his meal.

***

The next day, Petrus joined his teammates at Dock 10, where a banner read, "Welcome to the Olympic Village." There, the Badminton club cleared the floor and arranged cots and blankets. The Table Tennis club set up temporary walls and a clinic. Others hung banners and decorations.

Jeremy stood by an open cage filled with Olympic uniforms. Handing one to Petrus, he said, "Time to make an appearance."

Petrus stared wide-eyed at the perfectly-folded and spotless white uniform. The five Olympic rings sewn into the left breast reflected like glitter. Above them, the *Aldrintown* crest gleamed. Petrus thought, *this is really happening!* And then, Jeremy dropped a glistening ceremonial sword and scabbard on top, causing the uniform to fold in his hands. He clenched everything to his body as the sword dangled over his arm.

One of the twins said, "You gonna stare at it all day?" A startled Petrus clenched his gear together and followed them to change.

The fencers soon returned to the Village as a foursome, waving to those present. At first, Petrus waved with one hand, but when he saw the others wave with two, he copied them. *Do what they do,* he told himself.

They reached an open spot. Jeremy whispered to his teammates, "Ready for Salute." The twins moved on one side of Jeremy. Watching his teammates, Petrus ambled to Jeremy's other side.

Jeremy said, "Ready!"

Petrus' face began to hurt from smiling. Jeremy nudged him and whispered, "Sword!" Petrus shook and hurriedly grabbed the handle of his sword.

"*En grade!*" In unison, the four drew their swords and raised them high. Petrus looked upward into the glare of the sword. Nothing like the beat-up and bent sabres they used for training. Then Jeremy whispered, "At ease," and they all returned their swords smartly to their scabbards.

Petrus heaved a huge sigh. He felt weightless, puffing his chest as Jeremy thanked everyone present before making way for the next team.

But later, Jeremy leaned over to Petrus and said, "Next time, draw your sword with your *right* hand."

***

They reached the walking track circumnavigating the City Level. The Track team was there, having just mounted the finish line. Nearer to the fencers, boys dressed in Mallian silver-gray serenaded their half of the track team with tin whistles and bodhrans. Further away, denim-blue clad Rockfords cheered the other half *a capella.*

Petrus turned to Jeremy seeking a cue to perform another salute. But Jeremy stood idly watching the twins head a few steps the other way, shouting down the hall toward a band of Orwells. On seeing them, they howled in bass and stomped their feet *ram-tam-tam*. The twins joined the chorus.

Petrus asked Jeremy, "Guess we aren't saluting here?"

Jeremy folded his arms and said, "No."

Petrus nodded and walked toward the Orwells, drawn by the chanting. He liked their music best. However, the Orwells returned only with glances and strange looks. The nearest one turned his back. Then the twins noticed him and one waved him back toward Jeremy. Petrus gasped. Apologizing, he put both hands out and retreated.

He felt Jeremy pull him by the arm. "Not a good idea," he said. When Petrus asked why not, he said, "You don't just walk up to another clan like that."

Jeremy ushered him further away. "I keep forgetting you're still in school, right? How much do you have left?"

"A year."

"Ok, like in school, everyone gets along, right?"

"Yeah."

"It's not like that out here. Clans stick together." Then, invoking the slang for municipal, "You're a Muni, ok? You stay with Munis."

This stunned Petrus. "My parents said I shouldn't think like that."

Jeremey shook his head. "Your parents run all the life support. They keep us all alive. They are everyone's friend. You're not."

Petrus was stunned. *No, not true,* he thought. Whenever he accompanied his mother around the city, everyone greeted them. Everyone asked him how he was and remarked how much he grew. Didn't matter which clan.

Jeremy signed. "Sorry about that. But you've got a lot to learn. See this?" He opened his jacket just enough to show he wore his Scheemite tunic underneath. "This is who I'm competing for."

They waited patiently for the twins, who only returned after a public announcement called the Olympians to please gather in the Square.

***

Among the wide corridors leading to the Square, volunteers erected bleachers, set up venues, and mounted Olympic decorations. The fencers passed the volleyball courts and reached the fencing venue. The club was there having just finished setting up the two pistes. The older members present hastily assembled the excited kids so the Team could render a salute.

Jeremy spoke what the others were thinking, "Where's Michael?"

Petrus heard a muttered response from the twins, "Another Flettern screw-up." He turned toward them but could not tell who said it.

Jeremy whispered, "Not here. People are listening."

Reaching the Square, they followed the instructions of a city official to a marked spot in front of the statue of Buzz Aldrin in front of City Hall. But Jeremy said the Team had to do something first. He pointed up to the balcony of City Hall and told the official, "Our coaches are up there."

As Jeremy waved, the two armed guards on the balcony waved back while holding their weapons firm and steady. Jeremy brought the team around the statue to Salute them.

Petrus asked him what was happening. Jeremy explained that the Flettern leadership were meeting with the mayor about the most recent mishap on the surface. "Wouldn't want to be up there. Or be a Flettern about now."

One of the twins remarked, "Or ever."

Petrus recoiled. "Why are we talking like this? Things bad enough? I mean, Harland. He was our friend. Right?"

The twins bowed their heads and looked away.

Jeremy said, "He was our teammate. He won us our last medal." He nodded as though wanting to say more. Nothing further came.

They returned to their designated spot as the Minister of Health arrived to address the athletes as everyone in the Square gathered to watch. He began with a request for a moment of silence.

Petrus thought only about Harland and paid no attention to anything else. Harland was more than a just some teammate. He was an inspiration. Never did Petrus recall him acting as a Flettern, or treating anyone differently because of the colors of their tunic. A tear welled in his eye as he could not reconcile the truth, that the young man was gone so suddenly. It wasn't fair.

The sudden dispersal of the athletes startled him. The Minister had finished his speech and departed. Everyone went their own way. A trio of pretty Scheemite girls approached and surrounded Jeremy. The twins walked off with friends from other teams toward a gathering of ram-tamming Orwells.

Petrus watched them all go. He looked around, looking for someone to come to him. To give a pat on the back, or word of encouragement. But there were no other municipals there.

He gave up and headed away from the Square.

A few nearby Fletterns whispered among themselves and returned accusing stares that penetrated Petrus like the business end of a foil. Petrus recognized the tallest among them as Anthony, a friend of Michael's. He stepped into Petrus' path with his fists clenched and said, "Hey, you! . . . How'd you take our spot?" The others followed behind him.

Petrus asked, "Your spot?"

"Yeah. Michael should be wearing that thing."

"But, I beat him."

"You didn't lose your friends from working, either. One of us should be fighting for their honor. Not you."

Petrus wanted to tell them his father was down there too, but a trio of armed security guards marched past. The Fletterns quietly retreated but not without shooting him cautionary glares. Petrus raced home another way.

***

The apartment was again empty. With Anthony's words ringing in his ears. Petrus ripped of his white uniform and threw it to the floor. Then, he felt his bare chest. *Darn, my clothes are at the dock!* He flung upon his dresser drawer, and grabbed a green tunic. He listened intently for any sound coming from outside the door. Anything that meant those Flettern kids were waiting to make good on their threat.

Was a threat any way to show honor? To take away what I earned? To make me scared so I would give it up? The fear drained away from his face. Clenching his fists, he resolved not to run next time.

On the Screen, message icon flashed. It was from his father, a heavy-set man with very dark skin and bright eyes. Only the eyes were half-closed, and the usually jolly belly sagged as he leaned forward, propping himself on his elbows.

Petrus' jaw dropped. *Dad, what happened?*

"I just heard the news about you making the team. It made my day. Really, it did. I know I don't sound excited, but I'm so proud of you. I'll follow it while I'm down here. I promise. Now, just so you know. You heard what happened here, I'm sure. The accident happened right after I got here. Three dead now, one more went this morning. Everyone's worried, upset. Worst is over, I think, but it's tough here now. It's good the Games are there. Maybe it'll give everyone something to cheer about. Take their mind off things. So look proud. Remember what I told ya. Don't matter if you win or lose, but how you play the game. Please don't worry about me. I'll be fine."

Petrus went straight to the Newsfeed. "Three Fletterns to Replace Their Fallen Comrades." And there was Michael. One of the three.

At first, Petrus thought, *there goes our alternate.* But then he wondered what Michael must be going through. Losing his spot on the team. Now he's headed straight down into a deathtrap that claimed his mate. Would the next death report have Michael's picture?

He replied to his father, then returned to his room and picked up the uniform. Rubbing his fingers over the city crest, he recalled how graceful Michael took defeat. When duty called, Petrus imagined Michael saying, "I'll do it," without complaint. During the Games, Michael would be in quarantine, conditioning his body to handle life on the surface.

He returned to the Screen and sent a message to Michael, wishing him luck and safe return.

***

An announcement blared, *Warning! Ship on final approach at Dock 5! Warning! Ship on final approach at Dock 5!*

Jeremy said to Petrus, “Okay, here they come.”

Petrus thought of meeting the competition. Indeed, the thought of *visitors* coming to the city! Other kids his own age. Petrus never saw a kid from another city before. Would they be like aliens? He breathed deep and fought to keep his legs from shaking.

The huge bay door opened. Behind, waiting in formation, stood a well-dressed and mannered contingent wearing bright blood red. A photogenic young man led them, holding the flag of the South Astran capital.

Jeremy said, “See you later.” He greeted the leader of the contingent with a handshake, and then brought him toward the Olympic Village. The athletes marched behind in two perfect columns, trailed by a small army of bright red cargo-bots carrying their equipment.

Following them was Petrus’ assigned contingent, *Kennedysborough*, known as “K-Town,” sometimes pejoratively. They were the perennial doormats.

The K-Towners numbered half the capital continent. They limped from the ship in a gaggle. They wore uniforms of faded royal blue, some with white splotches and torn red trim. They lugged their bags by hand.

Petrus panned toward the other contingent walking away with Jeremy, who relished in the company. With a sigh, Petrus approached the K-Towners, introduced himself to the leader, and reached out his hand. Although the leader shook firmly, he gave only a bleary smile and said, “Loooong trip.” Petrus offered to carry his bags, but he declined.

He led them to the Village, where they immediately went to their designated cots, dropped their gear, and collapsed. Beyond them, the capitals puffed their chests and sneered at the K-Towners. Jeremy laughed with them.

Petrus avoided Jeremy's glance. With the K-Towners asleep and nothing else to do, he retreated.

***

The Olympic "Torch," a huge light bulb, was over. With it, the opening ceremony was over and the Games begun.

Jeremy arrived at Piste #1 for his first match. Petrus and the twins stood nearby. Behind them, dozens of Scheemites massed, cheering their hero. Not many from the other clans were there.

Petrus asked where the Coaches were. One of the twins replied that the Mayor needed them and they would not be around much. He then yelled to Jeremy, "Slice him up good! Get us started!"

Jeremy smiled and donned his mask.

Across the piste stood the K-Town team, gathered around their visibly smaller competitor. All of them rubbed his shoulder and chatted up a storm, encouraging and challenging him. Then their Coach said, "Let's go!" and pushed him forward.

Jeremy stood tall and strode onto the piste like a musketeer. He glared down at the opponent, mocking his lack of stature. Once the referee tested the gear, the combatants saluted and the crowd hushed.

"Fence!"

Ten minutes later, the match ended. A stunned and dejected Jeremy walked off, past the twins and Petrus without removing his mask or saying a word. His clansmen parted like the Red Sea to give way, then followed him with their heads down.

The twins stayed seated, covering their mouths with their hands. One of them muttered, "It's up to us, now."

Petrus watched the K-Towners, that ragtag bunch that looked so dead the previous night. They mobbed their teammate, yipping and hollering in celebration. Their

Coach celebrated with them, and then ushered them away from the piste. Petrus stayed watching them until the competitors for the next match arrived.

***

Down 1-6 in his first match, Petrus took his one timeout. His opponent, a capital, raised his arms and egged on his supporters. Petrus sat down next to Jeremy. The twins were off somewhere else.

Petrus rolled the mask off his head and on to the floor, and then pulled his hair with both hands.

Jeremy said, "It's your first match, and he's a tough opponent." But Jeremy's own disappointing loss still stung, sucking the air out of his words.

Petrus did not respond. Jeremy stayed quiet.

Loud screams.

Curious, Petrus craned his neck toward the other piste. It was the K-Towners again! Another member in a tight battle. Spying a Screen overhead broadcasting the match, Petrus saw how close the team gathered, nearly encroaching the piste, straining and groaning with each movement. The Coach pumped his fist, yowled his frustration, clapped until Petrus thought his bones would shatter. "Stay cool! You got this! Keep your head!"

The referee called to Petrus, "Son, timeout's over."

Petrus gave Jeremy a final glance, but his captain gave only tepid encouragement as he rested his chin on his hands. Petrus donned his mask and took his position. But his opponent's sensor failed, and the referee signaled for assistance.

Petrus felt the air leave his lungs and his hand grow limp. *Oh, let's just get this over with.* But the shouting of the K-Towners continued and drew Petrus' attention back to that Screen. The K-Towner had fallen behind, but his teammates kept shouting, kept applauding every touch. Their Coach's voice boomed over all the noise, "Relax. It's not over. Not over!"

"Relax. It's not over," Petrus said to himself.

But the mask muffled out the Coach's voice. In its place emerged the voice of Harland. He was back to that first lesson, facing a taller club member, barely able to hold the sword. "Relax," the voice kept saying.

The referee signaled *en garde*. Petrus swallowed.

"*Fence!*"

Within two seconds, Petrus won a clean touch.

And then again.

And again.

Petrus did not win, but he earned a "nice comeback" from his opponent when they shook hands.

Jeremy clapped as Petrus returned to the chair. "That was awesome. Good job." But the words were dry, and Petrus only grunted in reply. As Jeremy walked away, Petrus turned back to the Screen, showing the entire K-Town contingent bear-hugging their defeated comrade. He watched as long as he could, longing to be there among them.

***

Petrus would win his next two matches. By the final round, three teams including *Aldrintown* and *Kennedysborough* were tied for second place. Silver was in reach but so too was failing to medal. Before their final matches, the twins approached City Hall and looked up to the balcony. Their Coaches were still there, on guard. The twins shrugged their shoulders to them. The Coaches only shrugged back. *We're sorry.*

Then the twins split their final matches, meaning that wins by Jeremy and Petrus could secure the Silver. Their matches would occur simultaneously in the last pair of matches.

Petrus' opponent was a K-Towner of equal size. With the twins' watching, Petrus tried to get ready. But the K-Towners were louder than ever. Petrus paced back and forth, trying to block out the noise. He put on his mask just to help him concentrate, but the muffled sounds of the Coach penetrated it. Meanwhile, he listened for any words of support from the twins. A few claps. That was it.

The match began. On the first point, the K-Towner immediately lunged, surprising Petrus. 0-1. And again. 0-2. The third time, Petrus expected it, casually pushed the sword aside and tapped the opponent's shoulder.

The Coach continuously clapped his hands like thunder. "That's alright! Alright!" His teammates stood arm in arm, eyes fixed at their friend and knees wobbly. The twins stood like statues. Petrus gave up turning to them for any guidance or help.

Each point thereafter followed the same script with the K-Towner lunging straight away. If Petrus parried, he would eventually score. If not, the point was over in a split second. But once Petrus forged a lead, the K-Towner took timeout.

Petrus approached the clapping twins. He scolded them, "How about *saying* something for once. Let me know you're here." He sat down by himself to rest.

But the K-Towners were louder than spaceships when launched. The noise and chaos caused Petrus' hands to shake. He tried to steady them, but lost the grip of his sword on the next point. They traded points from there, but Petrus felt his confidence dipping. The K-Towner started fighting smarter. At 7-7, Petrus called his own timeout.

Just then, Jeremy arrived with his fist in the air, followed by a huge cheering crowd of Scheemites. After looking at the score, Jeremy raced to Petrus. "Hey, you win, we get Silver!"

Petrus thought. *So we have the Bronze?* He glanced at a Screen displaying the overall results and the ran the numbers through his head. Indeed, *Aldrintown* was assured the bronze.

Petrus asked himself if the color of the medal really mattered. Was Bronze OK? He glanced at the K-Town Coach every chance he could. Because of that Coach, the opponent was fighting like crazy, scoring on will more than talent. Just like Harland had done for Petrus. These visitors were nothing like the supposed perennial doormats. They showed everything in the Olympic ideal that his own team did not. If anyone deserved Silver, it was them.

He would make the last two points look good.

"Fence!"

The K-Towner lunge missed so badly, Petrus didn't move. But the K-Towner went straight to the ground with a yelp. He tossed his sword aside and held his ankle.

The Coach raced onto the piste. "No, NO!" He could not get the boy on his feet again. Two teammates carried him off, and the referee declared a walkover.

Petrus felt himself elevated by two huge arms as his teammates mobbed him and whooped it up. But Petrus stayed fixed on the other team. He asked to be let down, dropped his mask and sabre and walked over.

Seated, the boy's eyes stayed closed and mouth hung open. He gnashed his teeth as a medic treated him.

"Hey, you OK?" said Petrus extending his hand.

"Yeah, I'm OK," the boy replied with his eyes half shut, reaching out his own hand. "Good match."

"I'm sorry, . . . I hate to win this way. You're really good."

"Thanks. You're good, too." A smile. "I want a rematch, ok?"

Petrus heard a deep voice to his right. "What's your name, son?"

It was the Coach.

"Petrus, sir."

The Coach put his hand on Petrus' shoulder, "I watched you all day, son. You fight well. Thank you for coming over. I mean that."

The warmth from the Coach's hand penetrated the armor and spread through Petrus' body, remaining long after the Coach pulled away, rallied his troops, and congratulated them on a first, a team medal in fencing. Petrus withdrew slowly as the K-Towners drew in a circle and let out a victorious cheer.

***

After the medal ceremony, the four fencers congratulated each other. Petrus asked what they would do next, and all three said that they needed to prepared for duty on the surface. Their Olympic days were done. Their adult lives of toil would begin. They departed to a changing area, removed their white uniforms and deposited them in a basket.

Petrus heard a voice. It was Anthony. “Hey Petrus, wait here.” He waved to someone out of view.

Five large Flettern men appeared through the crowd and stood in front of him with their arms folded. Petrus stepped back, wondering what was happened. But then their clan chief, a tall muscular woman, emerged from among them and walked up to Petrus.

“Congratulations. Well done. I just came from quarantine. Michael is in there as you know. And he told me you sent him a message wishing him well. I promised to pass along his thanks. It’s been a tough time for us, and I appreciate that you cared enough to write him.”

Petrus held the medal in his hand. “Thank you, ma’am. I did it for Harland. Everything I did was because of him.”

She sniffed. “I know.” She tapped him on the shoulder and left quickly.

Later, Petrus lay alone in bed, holding his medal. From the deck above came the muffled *ram-tam-tam* as the Orwells celebrated the twins’ victories.

He still had two years left to fence. Next year, the Olympiad would be somewhere else, and he would go. Maybe he could make that team act like the K-Towners. Maybe he could get them all to remove their tunics and wear the white.

Scanning the medal, he realized that he scratched away the paint on the edge, exposing the plastic underneath.

Tom Galvin *is a retired U.S. Army colonel and Doctor of Education in Human and Organizational Learning from The George Washington University. He spent much of his later career overseas in Europe, Africa, and the Middle East and has an accomplished non-fiction background, but his lifelong dream has been to write ‘serious’ science fiction, concentrating on social issues and professionalism. He lives in Carlisle with his wife of thirteen years, Veronica, and three boys.*

TERA'S EYES

by Teddy Maurer

"Aseret, you look like crap."

"Thanks, Adnil," I answered.

"No, really. What's going on with you?"

"I just have something on my mind. Thanks for bringing me home."

"Want to talk about it? I'm here for you."

"Nah. This is something that could change the rest of my life. I think I need a higher power to help with this one. But, thanks."

"Holy Jesus, that sounds ominous. You know I love you, girl. Let me know if I can help in anyway," Adnil shouted when I turned away from her car.

As I walked toward my house, I knew I was running out of time. The months were passing quickly.

Tera was leaving. She felt she had to go back home, where she had grown up. I had been patient, hoping a lasting relationship would develop between us, but with the news of her moving away, I panicked. I wanted to tell her I was in love with her, but what if she wasn't ready for more than a friendship? If I didn't tell her, though, I could end up a sad old woman with death-bed regrets. I needed divine intervention to help me and that meant one thing; nature. My angels always found subtle ways of talking to me while I was immersed in it.

With nature in mind, I quickly grabbed a few things and jumped into my pick-up truck. I allowed the steering wheel to guide me where I needed to go, and that was the farm where I had spent my youth.

I turned off the dirt road and followed a narrow path into a freshly baled field, sending clouds of dust into the air. The truck bounced over the ruts and stones as I slowed to a stop. I stared out across the field into the woods, then sat back and watched the dust sparkle in the sunlight as it resettled on the windshield and hood in a thin layer of powder. With a heavy sigh, I grabbed my Stetson and stepped onto the field.

The pungent aroma of dried alfalfa hung heavy in the heat of the day. The scent took me to a time before my life took an ugly detour. I had made bad choices by allowing people into my life that didn't deserve to be there. Tera came into my life after I took the time to know and love myself again.

I had been introduced to her by a friend, Nho. I tried not to be obvious, but I couldn't stop staring at her. A white-gold aura surrounded her, and when I looked into her face to speak, I felt a warm flush rise up my body. Her smile blew me away, but it was her twinkling eyes that had me transfixed—not gray, not blue, but some color in between. I was swiftly and forcefully pulled into her gaze like a water falls rushing over a cliff. Faster and faster, I fell until my weight stretched me into a thread of light. A peace enveloped me as I glided by a great ball of brilliant light. It revealed to me the secret truths and knowledge of the Cosmos before I moved deeper into the unknown. There the power of the Universe trembled inside my heart and I burst into a billion atoms and coalesced into a new being. Was this a vision or an out of body experience? I don't know but whatever it was, on that day, I had died and was reborn.

I didn't run into Tera again until months later, where we exchanged phone numbers.

We began doing things together on occasion, and then we planned adventures—as friends—almost every weekend. I did ask her out on an official date once. She turned me down—said she wasn't ready to date again. I wasn't in a hurry. I was euphoric when I was with her and

I was a much better person because of her. I could subsist without her, but she was the center of my world and I felt fully alive when I was with her.

I leaned against the side of the truck, but quickly jerked away from its blistering hot metal. The sun was all alone in the cloudless sky; like an angry fireball, it smoldered. Shade was sparse, but the woods, along the opposite side of the field held a promise of relief. I reached into the truck for my satchel and began my trek toward the trees.

My heart opened to nature's music playing all around me. Its melody gave rhythm to the swarms of gnats dancing on the hot air currents above the field. Shrill, lovelorn, cicada solos, rose to a frantic climax then came to an abrupt silence. Bees buzzed in short bursts as they hurried from wild flower to wild flower. Butterflies bounced on hot air currents while crickets and grasshoppers scattered ahead of the toes of my boots in bursts. A brave grasshopper landed on my chest and pivoted like the hand of a clock to face me. It clung to my tee-shirt like a broach as I walked across the field to an adjoining wetland meadow. Near the tall grass of the fence row it kicked against my chest and flew off in a flash of brown and white.

Amid the patches of Cat o' nine tails and Swamp Sunflowers was a small tributary stream that fed into Schwaben Creek. It wasn't much more than a puddle at some spots—a slow trickle of water across bent grass, but it held deeper pools along its winding path where I discovered remnants of an old spring house; a crumbling stone foundation. I paused to dip my hands into the man-made pool and splashed the cool water onto the back of my neck. I thrilled at the shiver it sent through my body. To my delight, when I opened my eyes, Tera's face rippled in the pool of water beneath me. Our reflections danced on the water until they morphed into a single image—mine.

I plucked a nearby stem of wild Timothy hay and stuck it between my teeth. Its sweet juices took me back in time to the thoughts of the little girl who once lived there. I remembered Blue Bells that used to bloom along this stream when I was a child. I often picked a handful as a surprise gift for my mom.

My father had planted the majestic grove of pines before me. I closed my eyes briefly and inhaled the exhilarating scent of fresh hemlock. They had grown tall and thick. Good cover for the forest animals in the winter and shade in the heat of summer. I smiled because my father would be very proud of the little twigs he lovingly cared for. He would have liked Tera, too. With a twinkle in his eyes and a sheepish grin he would have teased me like an eight year old, with the clichéd song, "Arseret and Tera, sitting in a tree, k-i-s-s-i-n-g."

The shade of the pines was deep and cool. The thick layer of needles beneath the pines kept the underbrush from growing. This was the perfect place to sit. I pulled a sketchbook from my bag and I drew the beauty surrounding me onto its pages. But as I drew, I realized I was portraying the pain raging inside me on the pages. My sketch was filled with harsh angles and dark shadows. I had been mumbling under my breath, but not in prayer. I had been cussing. As clouds drifted in and the sun slowly dimmed, a wind gust stirred up a small dust devil that swooped across the field. Then a quiet hung over me. A storm was coming. I could smell it.

I sat quiet, feeling sorry for myself, wanting the storm to drench me. I wished it would soak me to the bone. I wanted it to pour into my heart and wash away the stains of sorrow living there.

A twig snapped close to me. I wasn't alone under the trees. A doe and her fawn stood a few yards from me. They both watched me and sniffed the air. Momma stomped her hoof but didn't flinch when I told her I wouldn't hurt them. They settled into the space and nibbled at the pine boughs overhead. I gently put the drawing pad into my bag, swung it over my shoulder and slowly stood up. The doe trotted closer and stopped mere feet from me. She watched me with her soft brown eyes. I whispered to her, telling her she was beautiful. She licked her nose, flipped her tail and threw her head into the air, but when I told her I wanted to stay under the trees during the coming storm, she slapped her hoof onto the ground and leaned closer, lowering her head, ears first. She stood her ground, making it clear, that this place was hers and I was leaving. I said a reluctant good-bye and stepped toward my truck.

Lightning flashed in the distance. I counted, "One thousand one, one thousand two, one thousand three, one thousand four, one thousand five," before hearing the rumble of thunder. Five miles away. The breeze had cooled markedly.

I took off my hat and reveled in a welcome rustle of wind through my hair. Birds and insects were preparing for the coming storm and many scolded me along the way for waiting so long to go to a safe place. Static in the air had the hairs on my arms standing on end. "One thousand one, one thousand two." The storm was getting even closer. The sky turned black, and huge drops of rain bounced off my shoulders. I ran the final distance to the truck, pressing my hat against my head to keep it from being blown away, and threw myself into the seat. I glanced back across the fields toward the pines where momma deer stood at the edge of the tree line. Lightning struck nearby and the thunder shook the ground. The doe disappeared under the trees.

Torrents of rain ran in ripples down the windshield. It washed the dust away in a matter of minutes, leaving me a clear view of the fields. The skies boiled overhead, turning a dirty yellow before turning almost black. Lightning struck, cutting the sky into jagged puzzle pieces and then boomed with the sounds of a hundred running horses overhead.

Rain fell harder and harder until I could barely see farther than a few yards in front of my windshield. The truck shook with each gust of wind. Was Tera out there in this storm? If so, I hoped she was somewhere safe. I wondered if she was alone or if someone was lucky enough to be spending time with her. I leaned against the head rest, closed my eyes and saw that she was safe. She told me she loved me and smiled at me from my day dream.

Thirty minutes ticked away on the dashboard clock while the storm raged. Then, with a sudden release, it quieted to nothing except water dripping from the trees and an occasional rumble of thunder as the storm moved down the valley. Through the smattering of leaves stuck to my windshield, I saw branches flung across the fields. Everywhere I looked, things were drooping or broken or under water puddles. The sky remained gloomy with its yellow gray cast.

I sucked in a deep breath and exhaled. I believed, in that moment, that I caused the storm by projecting my feelings of frustration and anger out into the Universe. What right did I have to send that negative emotion outward?

Was this the message my angels wanted me to hear? That Tera needed to move on like the storm, certainly wasn't the answer I had hoped for, but I had to be respectful and not interfere. If she happened to fall in love with someone else, I knew I'd die inside, but I had to pray she'd find the one that would make her feel the way she made me feel. She deserved that joy. Maybe she'd realize that person was me all along.

The thought of her not being in my life anymore hit me like a brick in the stomach. I felt sick inside. I stumbled out of the truck for fresh air. The blood from my whole body seemed to have drained to my feet. I sat on the running board of the truck with my face buried in my palms and cried.

I sat, numb, for a while, looking across the fields. The sun sat low in the sky, but it was shining again. Birds were singing and the fields were alive with sounds and activity. Rain had washed the dusty haze from the air. All was calm and clear, as was the clarity in my mind. It didn't make me happy, but I knew I had to let Tera go.

The doe appeared a short distance from the front bumper of my truck. Where was her fawn? She stood, head held high like the regal queen she was and blinked her good-byes to me. I waved and watched her gracefully bounce across the field and into the woods. Saying good-bye was something I'd better get used to.

It was late; time to head home. I pulled onto the dirt road, followed it to the main road and paused to look into the night sky. As I looked up into the great beyond, I felt a familiarity in my soul. I recalled the wisdom passed onto me by the ball of light, that day, in Tera's eyes. While I imagined it was her eyes or her smile that captured me, it was instead the recognition of her essence. Tera and I are an eternally joined pair of souls from Heaven, spending mortal lifetimes in creatures here on Earth. Our experiences on this planet were teaching us lessons for our next lives, here and, ultimately, our forever life in Heaven. Our souls had touched in many human lifetimes before, and would again. If not romantically in this human experience, perhaps the next, or the next, or the one after that. I thanked my angels for an answer to my prayers, their patience with my weaknesses, and their permission to spend precious time with my beloved in this life cycle. I would wait for Tera for as many lifetimes as necessary because she is pure light and unending love and the strange magic of the Universe lives within her, forever.

Teddy Maurer *was born, raised and lives in central Pennsylvania. She sees beauty everywhere and expresses it artistically via visual art, photography and writing. She shares a home in Harrisburg, Pennsylvania with her furry bundle of joy, Joey.*

APHRODITE

by J.A. Thomas

I live every day of my life at the mercy of Aphrodite. This is a true statement. You see, Aphrodite is the name of my boat, and in that name I believe lays the cause of all my adventures.

Aphrodite picked me one day when I was much younger and I was first learning the ways of the sea. She sat on dry land, tilting to one side. Her hull was covered with moss, and there were a few cracks that appeared to be the cause of her permanent place on the sand. The bowsprit had been split in twain and her paint had mostly worn away, showing only splintered and worn wood. I had been searching for a boat to call my own, but my finances were an atrocious mess, being that I preferred to spend most of my free time whiling away at my favorite watering hole, The Rusty Oar. I was scrolling through ads online, hoping to find a steal when one caught my eye. It read:

The boat you have been looking for is now on sale. Call now to get your hands on her before she is gone!

I decided to call the number and I asked if there was a boat for sale. The man who answered said, "Sure enough." But then he asked me, "How do know about her?"

I said, "I saw the ad online."

The fella paused for a moment before asking, "Online what?" Then said, "Never mind. If you want her, come take a look."

Well I took a look, and she wasn't a beauty, but something inside of me screamed that I needed to take her home. We agreed on a price of almost nothing and shook on it before the man cocked an eyebrow and put his hand on his hip, fixing his eyes on mine.

"I'm not sure how you found out about Aphrodite, but I wish you all the luck in the world with her. She brought me nothin' but heartache the entire time I owned her. I don't think she liked me much. Maybe she'll like you better." He sighed, his whole body deflating as his shoulders slumped, turned and walked away.

Then me and a buddy went and picked her up the next day. Word got back to me that the man died about a week later. The grapevine said he was found in the indented sand of the spot where Aphrodite had sat, his hands were clasped to the center of his chest over his heart. Heart attack was the official cause of death, but over the years as I have gotten to know Aphrodite, I'm not so sure. She has a way of getting to people. I'm lucky we get along so well.

Today I am the proud Captain of that very same ship named Aphrodite, although she is a might better sight than the day I first laid eyes on her. She keeps my life interesting, and I keep her purring like the Goddess she is. Together we run a small business along the Atlantic Ocean where I cater to newly engaged couples, young and old, who want to celebrate their engagements. After all, what better ship can you find to celebrate your love than one named Aphrodite?

I have a couple coming in today, and if you would like to join me, maybe you might understand Aphrodite a little better. You're welcome to come along, but keep in mind you might be surprised by what you hear. I never know what to expect because every ride is different.

We'll be seeing a couple named Paul and Ellen. The gentleman called me a week ago and told me he planned to propose over breakfast, then take her on a boat ride to celebrate, with some intimate alone time. That is fine by me and Aphrodite. I hope Paul and Ellen are as pleasant as they sounded on the phone.

Paul and Ellen

A young woman came skipping down the dock, her hair bouncing around her ears, a full on belly laugh sounding from her lips. I leaned forward from my reclined position against Aphrodite's side to take a full survey of the situation. The woman was running. But at the far end of the dock, a young man with hair long enough to cover his eyes, moseyed slowly down in my direction. His hands were shoved in his pants pockets and his head was bowed down, chin resting on his collar bone. The young lady stopped abruptly a few feet shy of where I sat.

"Come on, Paul! I thought we were racing. Here I am all disheveled and laughing my head off, and you have barely moved! Come on!" She spun around on her heel with her arms spread wide and her head tilted up to the sky. She stopped and turned her attention on me.

"I'm sorry he's taking so long. He's extremely shy, and I had to pretty much drag him here, even though this trip was his idea. It's a miracle we ever even met. Thank the stars above for the internet." She turned on her heel, and half ran back towards Paul, who was slowly meandering his way down the pier.

"Come on, you silly goose," she said as she reached out and grabbed his hand. She started to tug him in my direction. He appeared to relent and began to walk at a more human pace as she continued to bounce along beside him. As they finally arrived, I stood up and offered my hand.

"You must be Paul and Ellen. Welcome to Aphrodite. I'm Captain Jamie."

"Hello, Captain Jamie!" Ellen yelled. She grabbed my hand, shaking it up and down as if she were priming a water pump. Paul's hands stayed planted in his pockets. He gave a slight nod that I assumed was his greeting.

"Well come on board, the both of you," I said, and gestured for them to move on towards the front of the boat.

I placed my hand on Aphrodite's side as the two climbed aboard. I felt the vibrations that were emanating from her. A chuckle escaped from between my lips as I stepped up and made my way to the bridge.

"Now you two settle on in up there. We'll be sailing off in a few moments. Make yourselves comfortable." I turned over Aphrodite's engine.

We started out along the dock and beyond the coast toward our waterway's special entrance. An archway of lavender and honeysuckle flowers hung in waves along the shore, filling the air with the mild yet sweet scents characteristic of summer. As we passed through the arch, the squeaking noises of dolphins began softly but gained in pitch the farther along we sailed. "Look," I said, pointing out to sea, "The dolphins are getting closer." I slowed Aphrodite down a bit as Ellen leaned forward trying to catch a glimpse of the dolphins. Paul sat, his body rigid and his head drooping.

"Come on, Paul, look!" Ellen called out, and pointed to the clear blue water. Reluctantly, he stood and leaned his head over the side of the boat. A dolphin broke through the surface and blew a stream of water directly into Paul's face. He stumbled backwards, spitting and coughing and wiping at his face, and then fell across Ellen's lap, landing on the bench beside her. Several other dolphins jumped up and blew water in our direction, thoroughly soaking both Paul and Ellen. Their shoulders shook with their laughter. They seemed to be enjoying this strange turn of events.

"Sorry about that," I yelled to them over the squeals of the dolphins playing around us. "Some strange things happen when I take people out for a trip."

"No worries, this is amazing!" Ellen yelled back as Paul sat up on the bench. He pulled Ellen in close to him. He dropped his head again, but this time his hands were linked with hers as they sat.

As Aphrodite cut through the sea, water slapped along the sides of the boat. I smiled as I hoped that the couple would continue to enjoy their trip as the water slapped harder and louder.

Ellen squealed as I saw the fish jump over the boat. Ellen slapped Paul's knee and pointed as the fish dropped into the water. A second fish jumped and wiggled for a moment in midair before falling back into the water. Ellen rubbed water out of her eyes and Paul stood up, which probably was an ill-advised idea. The third fish jumped up and appeared to pause, suspended in front of Paul's face. The fish twisted around and his tail slapped back and forth across Paul's cheeks several times before diving back into the water.

Ellen stood up, her mouth agape. Paul didn't move at first. His eyes were wide and he shook his head, then wiped at his face with the back of his hand. A fourth fish jumped out and kissed Ellen on her lips before flying back into the water.

The two erupted into laughter. "Did that just really happen?" she asked Paul.

"I think so! Why didn't we bring a camera? No one's going to believe this story!" They fell into each other and collapsed onto the bench, alternating between still moments of disbelief, then laughter.

I smiled to myself as I turned the helm to begin our return journey. Aphrodite puttered along through the foliage.

The croaking of the frogs rang out as we passed a bouquet of lily pads sprouting upon the surface of the water. I was not surprised when one of them jumped on board. The frog was fat, with long legs and a wide head. The fellow jumped across the deck and stopped in front of the couple. Ellen squealed again. "Oh, Paul, look at that ugly frog!"

"Well, hello there, little guy," Ellen said, and bent over, holding her hand out. The frog jumped up into her palm. He opened his mouth with a belch and dropped a ring in her hand. The frog quickly jumped out of her palm, across the deck and back to his lily pad.

Paul jumped up from the bench and crossed over to Ellen, wrapping his arm around her back and picking up the ring from her palm.

"Ellen, look!" he exclaimed. He held up the ring for a moment then dropped to one knee.

"I don't know for sure what's happened here today, but I'm feeling something I've never felt before. I, I think I feel . . . alive! We have been together for years now and I know I'm in love with you. I haven't asked you to marry me because I honestly feared you would say no. But whatever happened today, whatever magic was at hand, this is a sign that I should have asked you a long time ago. I can't believe it. Ellen, would you marry me?"

She began to cry and laugh simultaneously. She nodded, falling into Paul's arms.

"I will marry you," Ellen said, "as long as you promise to always laugh with me. I want to have as much fun with you for the rest of our lives as we have had so far." Ellen then fell against Paul as he slipped the ring on her finger.

"It fits perfectly and it's so beautiful." Ellen held up her hand.

They sat, wrapped in each other's arms as we made our way back to the dock. Paul's demeanor had entirely changed. He sat up straight, his hair was tucked behind his ears and his head was lifted as he stared from the sea to his beautiful bride to be. As I pulled in and moored, they stood up together and climbed off the boat, pausing to turn to me.

"Thank you, Captain Jamie," Paul said. "We will remember this for the rest of our lives. No one will ever believe this happened to us." Paul held out his hand.

I took his hand and shook it.

"No thanks are needed, and I had very little to do with it. If you want to thank someone, thank Aphrodite." I rubbed my hand along her side.

Ellen and Paul walked along the dock to the shore.

"Well, Aphrodite, you outdid yourself. I wonder what tomorrow's tour will be like?"

J.A. Thomas *lives in Central PA with her husband, two sons and her two dogs. She began writing fiction seriously in 2011 to provide a creative outlet that had been missing while she pursued her professional career as an IT Project Manager. She writes across different genres, including YA and adult versions of suspense, mystery, romance, and light sci-fi/paranormal. J.A. can be found online on her website www.jathomas-author.com or on social media @jathomasauthor on twitter or www.facebook.com/jathomasauthor.*

65381127R00104

Made in the USA
Charleston, SC
19 December 2016